Praise for Emily Veinglory's
King of Dragons, King of Men

5 Angels and a Recommended Read "Emily Veinglory is a personal favorite of mine, just for the fact that her writing is so exquisitely rendered; it's almost poetic"

~ Michelle, Fallen Angel Reviews

4 Cups "I found an enchanting medieval story that will forever have a special place in my heart. Ms. Veinglory proved she could tell a story that captures more than a reader's libido. I hope she makes her wonderful book into a series. Anyone looking for an awesome book full of intrigue will want to grab King of Dragons, King of Men."

~ Susan, Coffee Time Romance

"What's next on Veinglory's menu? I'm hungry already"

~ Joyce Ellen Armond, Science Fiction Romance Online

"King of Dragons, King of Men is a true fantasy tale that involves great magical beings and ordinary people in extraordinary circumstances. The story creates a believable magical but ordinary world that begs to be explored."

~ Sabella, Joyfully Reviewed

King of Dragons, King of Men

Emily Veinglory

A Samhain publishing, Ltd. publication.

Samhain Publishing, Ltd.
512 Forest Lake Drive
Warner Robins, GA 31093
www.samhainpublishing.com

King of Dragons, King of Men
Print ISBN: 1-59998-422-9
Digital ISBN: 1-59998-330-3

Editing by Jessica Bimberg
Cover by Anne Cain

First Samhain Publishing, Ltd. electronic publication: February 2007
First Samhain Publishing, Ltd. print publication: October 2007

Dedication

Dedicated to my mother...and the Internet, but mostly to my mother.

Chapter One

William sat scowling, awaiting an audience with his lord, the baron. The great hall was bustling with petitioners, servants, and sundry folk milling around in the general vicinity just because they could. William attracted very little notice from anyone, from highest to lowest; the dog that sat at his heel was more remarked upon. He scowled and nudged it away with one foot but it contrived not to notice and leaned back onto his leg. The damn thing had been following him for days. It was white with long shedding hair and an aristocratic look that only served to make William feel even more unkempt than usual. Besides that it had the most uncanny eyes, pale blue with the darkest and most perfectly round pupils that could be imagined, like pin pricks in a closed casket.

William's friend and foster brother, Sir Allen of Argent, dropped down on the bench by his side, beaming with good will. Being both naturally handsome and particular about his appearance—and not having just traveled for two weeks upon the dusty road—he looked dazzling. His garb was white, embroidered with scarlet and his cloak was black. His hair was golden like that of a fairytale prince and his face proportioned like an angel. In moments like these, William could almost bring himself to hate the man. Such moments were frequent enough to be a recurring theme in confession whenever they were together, but never lasted very long. Allen was just too well meaning and too good of a friend.

"Good to see you here, Will," he said, as if the meeting were entirely uncontrived. "Now at least there's one other person here who knows which end of a sword is sharp." He slapped the scabbard of his sword and leaned against William casually, reaching one arm about his shoulders.

William gave him a baleful glare before turning his gaze back to the raised platform where the baron sat, speaking in low murmurs to some of his more favored followers. William was actually quite comfortable with Allen's touch, but he could not help but feel that he should not be. The idylls of their youth were long over and with it went the closeness they once knew.

William had been waiting some hours and fully expected to bide where he was quite a while longer, until the baron had fully made his point. Allen's company would be a rather mixed blessing, as ever. He was a good comrade, but always prodding, inquiring and quietly admiring. William had no notion at all of how Allen, being all that he was, came to have no better object of affection. He had hoped that it was a notion that might have faded. After all, it had been four long and rather eventful years since they last saw each other, and longer than that since they had been together in the way Allen seemed to yearn for. Long enough for Allen's fancies to fade? The moment he saw Allen, and saw Allen seeing him, he knew that was a vain hope.

William had come directly to the hall with the grime of the road still upon him. He could smell his own sour sweat and the dark brown color of his tunic was covering up for more than it should. Now that he was sitting still, he was getting cold and his cloak was bundled up on the saddle of his patient mare outside. Of course, given his luck, if he left the hall to retrieve it the baron would ask for him immediately. And he was only a few such offenses away from losing what little remained of his inheritance. Oh, and wouldn't the baron love to have a few good acres and a modest title to give to someone more "suitable"?

"Well," Allen said with amusement. "Not pleased to be pulled away from that curly-headed wife of yours? I don't recall being invited to the wedding but I suppose I must forgive you for that. I am told it was a small and rather sudden hand-fasting, but if that was for the usual reason we'd all know about it by now, eh?"

"I wasn't called; I came all the same," William said, choosing to stick to the first of his old friend's many questions, direct or implied.

"A better knight than the old bastard deserves."

William winced at such undiplomatic words. He had always thought Allen too brash a man, too unconventional, but could not help but like him all the same. Allen was known and long tolerated for his ways, but William was walking an altogether finer line. He was holding onto the last shrinking rump of the family estates by the skin of his teeth—and his own father had been very much in disgrace before he died. Running off with the king's favorite mistress being the worst and last of his trespasses before he retired to rusticate upon the family estates.

"He is the baron, and I am his knight," William said with pointed simplicity as if all other facts flowed seamlessly from these two.

"Ah well, and he gave you a pretty wife... Go on it is your turn."

The baron had suddenly found time for him. William wondered whether his own estimate of the time he was likely to wait had been too uncharitable, or Allen's good standing was somehow acting to his advantage. The baron beckoned vaguely with one hand, not even turning from his conversation.

"Sir William of White Lady Tor," the page announced.

William stepped forward and bowed low upon his knee. "My lord Baron, I do humbly offer my services in your defense against the attack from County Serle." He made every effort to sound, even to feel, sincere in his affirmation but in the great stone hall his voice became small and was almost lost. He could only hope that this time he would do better at concealing his real feelings for the whoring, war-mongering old bastard. That Baron Hambly had made the first attack in the current conflict, in a blatant land grab, was best not mentioned.

The baron looked down in mild surprise as if he had forgotten that the distant White Lady estate supported a man who might call himself a knight, or he disbelieved it. He still, no doubt, remembered their last meeting when the baron had been in waiting for his title and William a callow youth, yet to learn the virtue of caution. The baron had said some things about William's mother that did not bear repeating, and William had said some even less charitable things in return. The baron's insults had been commonplace but young William's were far more strident and amusing enough to be long remembered by many who were present—not least the baron himself.

At last the baron spoke in low and disdainful tones. "It is good to have your sword, late as it comes, William," he said grudgingly and with obvious disinterest. "You may join the rest of my forces." His need for swords apparently outweighing any personal animosity he might feel, for now.

William backed away, hoping that his emotions did not show clearly on his face. The baron had not bothered to refer to William as "sir" although those spurs had been conferred more than five years ago during a brief stay at court. And "late"? William had not even been informed of the baron's over-hasty venture and would have rallied immediately if he had. He might have little respect for the man, but he owed the title his full

10

allegiance. William made a silent bow, and cursed himself as he turned his back perhaps a little too soon for proper respect—he could only hope the baron's attention had been diverted before that moment.

He was met towards the back of the hall by Allen who clapped a hand upon his back. "Come to my tent and share a glass. It has been far too long since I saw you last, and I am a little aggrieved that it took a battle to bring us together again."

William complied mutely. It was Allen's letter that had drawn him hence; Allen saw a hard battle ahead and wanted his childhood friend by his side. He had not been so gauche (or indiscreet) as to write that exactly, but he must surely have known William well enough to know he would offer his services as knight, if they were called for.

William was a little tired of dancing to other people's music, but he understood Allen's situation. Allen's family was old and proud, but he a second son. He took his brother's money and stayed in return, well clear of their estates. He found his way into almost every skirmish, tourney or ball within the realm. Allen was everyone's image of a knight with his golden looks and winning ways, glossing over his lack of personal land or title. Sometimes, it seemed, Allen got a little tired of his usual company—men who did well at arms but had precious little for brains—and he would contrive some way to pull William into his schemes. If anything, he had shown great restraint over these last few years in not making contact on the basis of friendship alone.

If only William could use this opportunity to repair the baron's opinion of him, after all in their last conversation William had been a most naive and over-opinionated youth. The baron should surely understand his rash comments at that time had been but youthful foolishness? William could only hope so. He was unsure, however, how to undo the damage without retracting the content of his ripostes. If there was one thing he would defend more vigorously than his fiery mother, it was her memory now that she was nearly ten years gone.

William and Allen walked together to his pavilion; it was as large and white as the sails of a great boat. At least Allen's brother was still providing the coin to support a life with some comforts. They walked into the cool interior, with Allen stepping lightly ahead. He waved vaguely to the center of the room where a bed and chair sat on either side of a low table upon which chessmen were placed ready for a game. He went to a cabinet to one side and opened it to reveal a crowd of bottles and engraved goblets. Allen was obviously completely at his ease, and his assurance began to dissolve away William's own precautionary reserve. Cliché that it was, it was as if they had never been apart.

Now his own unfortunate wife, Margaret, might leave the room for a moment and return a stranger—but four years had put no distance between him and Allen. This was not a complete relief, as William had never entirely resolved how to behave around a man he loved as a brother, but who (inexplicably) loved him as rather more than that. William's maturing mind had grappled with church prohibitions and finally put aside any unchaste expression of their bond, but deep down there was much in that intimacy that he missed, and mourned.

Allen poured wine. "So dour for a newly married man," he quipped, but there was an edge to his voice that William did not care for.

"A favor, Allen—no two," William snapped.

"Of course." Allen said that with absolute veracity as if he would give his life to William upon request. Which, given the type of man he was, he very well might. Allen's flippant demeanor belied a heart that was most seriously and disarmingly chivalrous. After all, any normal man would be offended at being spoken to in such a tone.

William barely managed to cling to his churlish intent. "Say nothing more about my wife," he said. "And say nothing about saying nothing."

Allen's habitual smile fell from his face, and he looked on frozen for a while. It made William feel most discourteous, but not enough to retract the request. William was well aware that this reflected more on his own intractable stubbornness than anything else. Allen, not for the first time, merely reassumed his amiable expression, and passed William a goblet.

"Well enough," he said casting around for another topic to speak about... "A fine new hound you have."

William looked down to his heel where the white and wolf-like creature was still most ardently following him. "It took up with me upon the road," he said diffidently. "And it is well-mannered enough. I only worry that someone is missing it. It would do me no good to be accused of theft on top of everything else."

"Oh, William," Allen chided. "Always questioning good fortune. Just don't start questioning *me* again. Creatures like that beast and me take to you because we care to, for better or ill, and I can only commend the beast's taste. That said, you will stay with me of course—until we move to the field of combat."

"I really couldn't..."

"...refuse," Allen interrupted. "You really couldn't refuse. Not without insulting me greatly."

William shrugged noncommittally and drained his glass, knowing that his belongings were probably already being moved. Not that this would be a time-consuming process. He had brought only simple things. Allen refilled his glass with a quick look of concern and some pleasure.

"Come and play a game with me," he said. "I can find no decent partners here."

William was pleased to do so, although he gave his friend a chastising glance for the way he had said "partners". Allen had always had a fey manner, with habits to match, but William did not choose to encourage it. One day he feared his old friend would act too outrageously for the nobles he depended upon to indulge—or for his brother to continue his patronage.

William was pleased to have Allen safely across the chessboard, giving him some rules to play by, even if in only the most limited sense. He sat upon the edge of Allen's sleeping pallet and Allen took the chair. William looked across at his old friend, only a little older than him, yet somehow so much...more. How he envied the ease with which Allen wore his privileges, his good looks and his sunny character. Allen was smaller than William, yet better proportioned, and looked more like a mythical king than a vavasour knight. His only flaw being an irrational attachment to his foster brother...and a general tendency to dally with men rather than maids. He did so discreetly though, so that no harm had come from it, so far. It would take a hard man indeed to hate Allen, by any cause.

Allen carried the conversation about their childhood adventures and the current coils of intrigue winding through the court—the grand court of the king as well as the more local baronial scene. There was, as usual, a gaggle of mistresses and men all fawning upon the baron and, those who could, upon the king. William kept his eyes mainly upon the pieces, and made only the briefest acknowledgement of Allen's chatter. He won two games easily, and they were upon the third as dusk drew near and a group of young knights called for Allen to visit the taverns with them. He merely waved them away with a ribald joke, ignoring their curious looks and the murmured explanations by those from their neck of the county.

"Black Will his foster brother."

"Bring him also."

"He will not come."

Dour William, black of hair, and black by nature—they were not the first to note it. William was meant to gain a little noble gloss staying with Allen's family during his youth. William's father was hampered in the task of raising a noble son by the fact that the king was likely to kill him if ever they met again. Actually, William's character proved to be made of sterner stuff and resisted any molding even if it was intended for his own benefit. All that had been gained was that two boys with very different natures had learned to tolerate, and eventually appreciate, each other's company.

"Idiots, but well-meaning," Allen said by way of apology, filling William's cup again

"You'll get no more out of me with drink," William warned, trying to figure how much he had drunk already, and how long it was since he had eaten.

"No? And are you so sure I have an ulterior motive?" At William's blank gaze he merely shrugged. "Well, it's good for what ails you. Which this is not."

Allen tipped the board so that the finely carved pieces fell to the floor. William bent to recover the ivory queen, her regal scepter held high. Even that modest movement made his vision blur and the billowing walls sway counter to their usual motion. Was that the second bottle, surely not the third?

"Let it be," Allen snapped.

He reached forward and covered William's hand with his own. William snatched his hand back as if it were burned, and stood suddenly. Allen stood also, putting his hands on William's shoulders, looking him directly in the eyes.

"Will," he said. "You have made yourself clear on that matter. I would never..."

"I know, I know," William muttered, abashed by his reflexive action. "I swear it is just that I am on edge, and..."

He was dizzy and blinked his eyes to try and clear his sight, having apparently drunk far too deeply from his much-replenished glass. He swayed and would have fallen had Allen not caught hold of him. William let himself lean in slightly, smelling the faint musk of Allen's body. Older memories welled up within him. Their bodies wound together in the eave of the old barn, discovering joy of guiltless passion during long, stolen summer afternoons. What had he lost in loving so? He had never found the like of it again.

"You've had a hard journey, little brother, perhaps it's time we went to our rest." Allen sat him back on the pallet, then scooped up his feet and put them up on the bed. William looked foggily up at Allen, little able to move but hardly willing to steal a man's bed.

"Allen I can't..."

"...disappoint your brother by refusing his hospitality. I'll have a separate pallet set up for you, but tonight this will have to do."

William's thoughts were too fogged to disagree and suddenly he was so tired. Some part of him was mildly annoyed that Allen was still finishing his sentences, as if he owned half his thoughts. They'd had time to grow up, to grow apart—it was strange that it had not happened. His eyelids slid down as if the weight of the world was on them. Fickle consciousness slipped far away.

Chapter Two

Allen lay, still trying to ignore the breaking day, watching the light play across the fabric of his pavilion. Truly there were worse things than to be lying abed and embracing a pretty man. Except of course that Will took rather more than his share of the bed, the embrace was chaste, and within days they might both be dead upon the so-called field of valor. He sighed and raised his head a little to look at his foster brother.

He had been tormenting himself with visions of William cavorting with his new wife and engrossed in the renovation of his old family estate—recently made his own. Now he found Will thinner and gloomier than ever, and felt guilty of his resentment. Better in truth that it had been so, even if it meant he lost his dear friend's company and (such as they were) his affections.

He had kept William frequently in his mind's eye, but had still forgotten much. The uneven harmony of his features, the depth of his black eyes, the way there was always ink staining his fingers, and a slight scholar's hunch to his back. Better, perhaps, if William had pursued his books rather than fought so fiercely to be the knight his parents would have raised, had they but lived. Ah well, it is better not to tempt the fates. Young Will would have only pursued them straight into a monastery—

and been one of those monks who actually observed his vows. *Settle for friendship*, he admonished himself. *It's a rare enough gift at that.*

The baron's page entered, and his eyes went a little wide at the scene. Allen knew he had been caught looking at his bedmate with rather more than proper disinterest. That would do his own reputation no noticeable amount of harm but Will would be less than pleased if rumors began to fly. Well, nothing for it now—denials only compound a gossip's certainty.

"Um...Sir Allen," the page stammered. "The baron requests the presence of yourself and Sir William... Is that he?"

"It is." Allen sighed. "And you may consider us told."

"At your earliest convenience, my lords." The page bowed, although not very low, and backed away.

Allen spent one short moment saying farewell to warmth and comfort, and then peeled himself away from both. He bent and patted William on the side of his cheek.

"Rise and shine, the baron summons."

William blinked blearily and moaned, but where others might gripe and complain he merely clenched his teeth and stood, feeling about for his boots and sword.

"No questions?" Allen asked.

"The baron wants us; seems clear enough," William mumbled as he splashed water from the basin on his face.

Allen looked out at the day and selected a woolen cloak bordered with golden irises. They both dressed and then Allen took the lead and they walked together through the waking camp to the hall where the baron waited. Baron Hambly lolled deep in his sheepskin-padded chair.

"Come here, you two," he said.

The room was bare except for servants, a table crowded with maps and the baron's youngest son, Sir Piers.

"Sir Piers wishes to see whether Serle is massing already at the field of combat. It is too early to do so with honor but there are reports... You shall go with him."

Allen smiled and bowed his obedience, internally cursing an early ride, and as mere entourage to this over-privileged youth. Piers was not yet twenty, red-haired and pale, and with confidence beyond both his years and his capabilities. No doubt he would see this as a chance to demonstrate his courage, and do something foolhardy to risk all their lives. Allen did not doubt his own bravery, but he was greatly averse to gambling his life without some kind of good reason.

They followed the young knight to the horse-line where he selected from his many fine mounts. Allen considered himself lucky to have two sound steeds, mainly against the possibility than one might sicken or be killed. William, he noticed, had the same stolid mare that Allen's father had given him many years ago. A good mare, but aging now as the white whiskers about her muzzle and her drooping lip declared. They got ready for the foray in silence, knowing not to speak before Piers invited it.

The younger man waited impatiently as they prepared and mounted.

"This way," he commanded curtly and spurred away.

Allen caught William's eyes and shook his head, smiling. They followed at a more leisurely pace. The first fires were being rekindled and the men rose shaggy-headed and surveyed the day from their tent flaps. Some looked sharply to see two knights riding, but seeing no armor they quickly turned away. Until the predetermined day of the battle, they were in little danger of attack. Piers probably eschewed his mail to show bravado. Allen knew the day would warm as it passed, and he was not encasing himself in iron without good reason.

They rode away from the camp on one of the foot-worn marked paths. The horses flicked their tails, but settled to a swift walk, reined back from breaking to a trot. They followed Piers' lead, towards the distant tree line. It seemed sensible to Allen that if the enemy were moving troops in secret it would be in the cover of the forest. He looked back to see William plodding behind, his white hound running obediently behind.

Piers spoke no more as they traveled, even as they entered the woods. It irked Allen to follow a man who communicated so little and could hardly be counted on to act wisely by his own council alone. A man with rank, however, was not required to act wisely, and a dispossessed second son would gain nothing by objecting.

He tried to ride alert. He scanned for a glint of metal or movement against the wind, his nose questing for horses or smoke—to no avail. When fortune turned, it did so on an instant and Allen was quite unprepared. They followed the slope of the terrain and came suddenly upon a small party, also moving amongst the densely growing birches.

The enemy party consisted of one knight upon a horse and two other men on foot beside him. They were archers and immediately raised the bows. Piers' horse reared and darted sideways, the movement making him fumble as he reached for his sword. Two hastily released arrows flew, he did not see where. Allen swore and drew his own weapon, but slower than the other knight who spurred past him, after Piers. He had no glimpse of William and dared not waste the time to turn, but charged at the archers before they could release another volley. They backed up nervously and drew their swords but Allen hacked one down; the other ran. Allen grimaced and gave chase. He could not risk the archer stopping under cover and turning the lethal longbow on them again.

Precious minutes later he retraced his path, his blade bloody and his horse puffing clouds of mist. He could not be certain either man was dead, but they would not fight again this day, and that was enough to waste no more time on them. He heard a clash of metal and cantered forward towards it, weaving dangerously through the trees and letting the branches whip him as he passed.

At the head of a small ravine, he looked down, and saw William slip off his horse and dodge around the enemy knight's white-footed mare—unlucky for this owner at least. William moved with precision, as he had practiced so often, knocking aside a weak attack and driving his blade forward like a spear. By the time Allen reached him, William was wiping his sword on his old brown cloak, and they turned together towards Piers. The boy leaned forward in his saddle, the spine of an arrow protruding from between his anguished fingers. It seemed one of the bolts had struck true after all. William looked grim.

"Start back with him," he said, easily assuming control. "I won't be far behind."

Allen bent over and grasped the bridle of Piers' horse and led it forward, hoping the young knight could stay in his saddle. The trees looked strange but Allen turned back in the direction of camp. He saw a familiar path, and by it the body of a horse. It was William's gray mare, a broken off arrow protruding from its eye. Allen frowned but did not let his confusion impair his action. He would know that animal anywhere and had now seen it two places at once; he rode on.

Before he was out of the trees, William was beside him. He had cut off most of the dead knight's armor and slung the body across the saddle before him. He rode his mare, the same

21

dappled coat, the same whorls, the same drooping lip beneath the same worn bit. Allen felt his blood run cold, and knew some of it must show in his face. How could there be two such horses?

"Anyone we know?" Allen asked, hoping that fear for a comrade from Serle might explain his pallor.

William shook his head, and they proceeded back to camp in silence again. The white dog, Allen noted, was nowhere to be seen.

Chapter Three

"A disciple of Ahriman?" Barrett the Earl of Serle asked with due concern.

Festrigan could see the weight of this new worry settle visibly over Barrett's bowed shoulders. The earl had enough to deal with in his neighbors and his enemies at court, without becoming embroiled in matters of gods and their influence. But a crucial crossroad was approaching and the least misadventure might put all of humanity upon a calamitous path to damnation. Festrigan hesitated, wonder how to best get Barrett to see things his way.

Festrigan nodded solemnly. "I am quite sure of it," he said. "A knight of a low station, by the name of William of White Lady Tor."

"Poor, and a knight? That does not sound like a like the sort of man to follow the devil."

Festrigan was used to Barrett's way of seeing the world. The poor were below notice, knights were virtuous, God's will was righteous and the king was to be served unto death. It was an outlook that had taken a hard knock a few years ago when he discovered that the king he had supported was illegitimate, but it seemed that once Barrett gave his loyalty he was loath to retract it. His support for King Harild remained unshaken, and in many ways it was more fundamental to his nature than his fear of God.

In his own quiet way, Festrigan struggled to convey some of the subtleties of his own views, fearing that he might easily give too much away. "There are many paths to Ahriman's service. He may not have sought it'"

Barrett glared moodily at his advisor. It was clear that he was not entirely willing to see the devil's minion as anything other than simply evil. He scratched absently at his ginger-toned beard and shrugged.

"Ahriman's involvement must be contained," Barrett said, obviously happier in contemplating action than pondering meaning. "This knight must be captured or killed. It must be a priority of the battle. For whilst this disciple draws Ahriman's attention to this realm, it cannot go well for us."

Festrigan could only agree with that. "I would prefer to have him alive, but in either case a victory for Baron Hambly would serve Ahriman's purpose better than if we were to prevail," he agreed. "And Ahriman takes a closer interest in his followers than our Lord of Light. Sometimes the freedom our good Lord gives us...is wearying."

Festrigan stood slowly and sighed. Wearying indeed when you could only try and fathom His wishes from scraps and clues, whilst Ahriman was known to speak to his followers directly. Festrigan ran his long fingers over his narrow chin in a gesture he knew to be habitual but could never shake. He hesitated to raise the issue that was on both their minds, but it could not go unconsidered.

Festrigan had long aided Barrett in his goal of supporting Harild as prince and king—Barrett had in return helped Festrigan search for the last great magical artifact left in the world. That goal being very far from achieved, much to Festrigan's dissatisfaction. Sometimes he wondered how hard the earl had really tried, when there was always some other folly he preferred to commit his men and funds to.

"Ahriman may be seeking a thrall," Festrigan speculated with reluctance. "A man to retrieve the Regent's Bridle. It bothered me enough that Hambly seized the land where it lies hidden, but even if he sought the Bridle, he had no way to find it."

Barrett leaned forward and rested his elbows upon the drafting table. Festrigan wondered how seriously the earl would take this possibility. He had often accused his advisor of having a most unhealthy obsession with the Bridle. Festrigan had racked his brain but he had never quite managed to convince the earl of the Bridle's true importance, hampered by his great reluctance to tell the whole truth about the matter.

The disputed lands were outlined upon the great map that lay before them on the scarred old table. It had been marked and redrawn by many different hands. The fresher lines showed the disposition of troops and the place of battle that had been mutually agreed. Others indicated buildings, walls, marshes and every kind of obstacle old or new. Festrigan had interrogated that old map with spells and pendulums and every conceivable device, but on the matter of the Bridle it remained stubbornly mute.

Festrigan placed his hand upon the back of the earl's chair. He had cause to notice that his was a remarkably gnarled hand, thin with age, with thick blue veins standing out in stark relief. Age in itself would not be such a worry, but he was one of the last people to know the full story of the Bridle and time was running out in terms of finding a solution.

He had not even told his oldest comrade, the earl, the full story of the talisman. He had told him, of course, that it was an item that gave its wearer the ability to detect whether a person was a direct descendent of the first king of all Ordran, Lukas the First. That was true enough and a cause for concern, as crowns don't always flow in the same direction as blood.

Festrigan stared down at his hand and grimaced. He had to find his own successor, against the chance that his own remaining time would simply not be enough. But in all this time he had never seen anyone that might want, or deserve, that mantle. It had little to recommend it bar a chance to save the world....

He turned his attention to the map, as if it might, somehow, miraculously show them where the Bridle, or for that matter the devil, hid. The damned Bridle had disappeared long ago after the thief bearing it was chased down the main road to the border and felled with an arrow, only to be found not to have it on him. It must have been disposed of somewhere along that small stretch of road that Hambly had seized, but an exhaustive search showed the land to be empty of people or tracks, and the Bridle had not been seen since. Festrigan had cast a few uncertain auguries and they all suggested the Bridle was still nearby, though no search ever uncovered it and the ground was now hopelessly churned and overturned. It was so close, so close.

Was it just a coincidence that this same road led eventually to White Lady Tor? He stored that idea away for future consideration. That house was known to be out of favor with the king and so might enjoy having the means to topple him. Such schemes might seem important to men like Barrett, but in truth they were just distractions. For although the Bridle could provide the means to topple a dynasty, there was more to it than that, much more.

"We must seize this knight," Barrett said suddenly, betraying the predictable course his thoughts had been taking. "We must know what he knows, by whatever means." He turned awkwardly to Festrigan, hampered by the stiffness of his bones. "I will instruct my best knights, those that I trust, to seek him out, and then I will place him in your hands."

"Mayhap this young knight can be reasoned with," Festrigan said softly.

"Or threatened, or tricked, or drugged...or needs be, tortured," Barrett replied more firmly. As so often happened, once the earl determined what he wished to happen he drove at it firmly and would not be dissuaded.

Festrigan's lips tightened, but he made no reply. He had never approved of the earl's ability to be ruthless when driven to it—even when it was obviously called for. He turned towards the door. Seeking his solitude, as he did so often these days.

"With your leave..." he murmured, and the earl waved his permission.

Festrigan left the earl's chamber and walked slowly to his own tower rooms. The winding stair to his lair was proving a greater challenge with every passing month, but he cherished and clung to the privacy it afforded him. There were many things in his rooms in that high tower that he would not wish anyone, not least Barrett, to see. He took the iron key from his belt and let himself into the dusty rooms. They were cluttered with a cornucopia of peculiar items, most clogged and covered in grime as no servants were ever admitted within. It was a lifetime's accumulation, and enough to hang him as a witch in almost any court in the land.

Amongst the gospels and works of philosophers there nestled grimoires and spell books, most of them the useless ranting of deluded men, but a few giving means to tap into the last scattered remnants of free magic in the world. Icons and relics lay beside fetishes and pagan amulets. Festrigan ran his hand over a clean, glossy covered edition of the *Contemplations of Phoselus* where it lay upon the highest surface of his bracketed bookshelf, almost more precious to him than the books of God's true disciples. It was Phoselus's writings that had first convinced him that magic properly belonged only to God. Miracles were a great wonder and blessing and well might the righteous revel in them, but similar powers in a man's hands lead inevitably to great evil.

These so-called sons of God who kept appearing, trying to lead humanity astray... There was no greater evidence of their origins than for the followers of Ahriman who arose here and there, causing troubles and chaos that took years to suppress. It was a great but necessary irony that Festrigan was forced to fight fire with fire, and this latest crisis only convinced him that he had been right to risk his soul in virtue's service. He had to know how to use the arts of magic if he was to stop the devil's peons from doing their worst. And their very worst would be to recover the Regent's Bridle and use it for its true purpose—to open the door into the land of demons and allow them and the magic that surrounded them back into the world of men.

It was as a young student that he first found accounts of the Bridle, its creation and purpose. He had found many other tales of it since from diverse sources, but many so carefully phrased that only a knowing eye would discern their meaning. But beyond that it was his heart, his soul, that knew the truth of it. Acquiring and securing the Bridle was his life's purpose. It was a great purpose, but he had so little life left to achieve it. If only this crisis had come sooner when he was a younger man more clear in his thinking and less set in his ways....

The world had stumbled down a largely virtuous course for some years and magic grew weaker with every passing year, robbing the devil of his favorite tools. There were a few extraordinary devices that retained their uncanny functions. One was the pocked sphere of volcanic glass that Festrigan drew carefully from the cabinet behind his desk. Its images were growing more scarce and faded, but this day it was willing to show him a glimpse of what he sought. God, no doubt, knew where the Bridle lay but it was His way to let people make their own fates. The devil might also know and so might his followers. The knowledge was almost within Festrigan's grasp.

The surface shifted, something moved and glowed palely at its center. Gradually he could discern a young man in earth-toned clothing sitting astride an old gray mare. He had first seen this man a short time before, with the devil's shadow at his shoulder. Now the shadow was darker as the taint struggled to deepen its grip upon this unfortunate mortal. There were other figures near him, too distorted to be clear. The image of the mare shifted, from normal beast to a spectral creature woven from bones, wires and leathery hide. As shadows flickered both aspects showed themselves through the stone's insight. It was the follower of Ahriman upon a devil-beast disguised as a horse. He hoped that even Barrett's best men would be up to the job of capturing him.

Festrigan saw the image dwindle and fade away. He covered the seeing stone with its usual cloth and whispered a cantrip to cleanse it and help its strength endure just a little longer. He only wished that he knew a way to strengthen his mortal form, but he had always held that magics were too dark to risk except in desperate straits. He went in search of the records that described them, it seemed that just such desperate times might now be approaching.

Even as he turned to other tasks he mused over the vision. The sight of the hell-horse bothered him. He had detected the tainted knight only the previous day and had assumed he was newly fallen. Such a man would be easily seized and might even turn willingly to the Light. But if he had already been given powers of his own... No, Festrigan shook his head and paused to stare contemplatively out his high turret window. All the tracts he had read and his own meager experiences suggested that the progression was gradual, and the stone still showed the knight as human—he had little power of his own as yet. The progression of a dark disciple was always slow, and almost always unwilling. There was time yet not only to learn what this man knew, but also to save him. Perhaps even to find a successor in God's service, for the man the devil chose must have strengths to him that could serve God as well, or better.

Curiosity was getting the better of him. Festrigan admitted to himself that he looked forward to seeing a follower of Ahriman in the flesh. He felt confident that his advantage of years, learning and secret arts would be enough to bend the young man from his will and steal him from the devil's service. But what he wanted most was that Bridle, the Regent's Bridle in his own gnarled hands.

Chapter Four

The meal that evening was heavy with the unsaid. William took his repast in Allen's company, by mutual assumption; for once William did not protest his friend's hospitality. William was numb, only half-aware of the tension to begin with, but as he tired of his disordered thoughts he became more aware of Allen's perturbed regard. Allen sat across the small table with the dancing flame of a single candle between them.

His enduring silence was an unusual and ominous sign in itself, but William was guiltily pleased that Allen was keeping his questions to himself; there were few questions he could ask for which there would be an answer forthcoming. William's wine glass sat full but untouched at his right hand, his plate disarranged but hardly lightened as time crawled by. It was strange how one small occurrence could upset the entire balance of his life—one small and totally inexplicable occurrence. William had always thought of himself as a man of principle, but now he was properly aware of the power of expedience in making a man accept aid from any quarter.

William was pleased that his friend had bidden the servants not to light the lamps or torches. Darkness suited him, his mood and his self-obsessed thoughts, and made it easier for him to avoid Allen's searching gaze. Over and over he replayed the action of the day. The first arrow fired in that brief skirmish had felled his old mare. It had taken her straight through the eye and she had fallen immediately to the ground, dead before she hit it. By the time he struggled clear of the tack and pulled his trapped leg from beneath her, Piers' horse had bolted and Allen had charged in pursuit of the archers. He had seen Piers rock in the saddle, wounded, and his first thought had been to go to the aid of the baron's son. But Piers' horse was swift and startled and he would not easily catch it, especially not afoot. William had stood alone in the suddenly empty clearing, wondering just what the hell he was supposed to do

He spared one more look at his stolid mare, so suddenly gone after so many years of faithful service. Then he turned to the middle of the clearing to see...a mare. She was identical to his old girl, right down to the hard worn and mended tack, standing and observing him placidly, but her eyes sparkled with more than the dull obedience of the real animal. The likeness was too exact to be anything but uncanny and any properly God-fearing man should have shrunk from her with prayers and protestations. Even William's well-trained and tutored mind could do no more than grope in the darkness for explanations, and he did not have the time to indulge it for long. He thought for a moment of the fairy horses that were said to come and steal away human lads who mounted them, but they were handsome and vibrant creatures, not battered old replicas. In the end it was not thoughts of God that guided him, it was consideration of the peril of his comrades which pushed down his superstitious terror.

She stood placidly at his approach, making neither welcome nor demure. He took the reins and put his hand upon the saddle, warm as if he had just now dismounted from it. He swung his leg over the creature with an assurance that he did not feel, and when it answered his commands, just like an ordinary horse, he almost fainted from relief. He must get to

Piers, and every other consideration must wait until the boy's safety, should that be possible, was secured. The death of the earl's son would seal his doom just as he sought to forestall it. Whatever the horse-that-was-not-a-horse might be must be risked for his sake. Not to mention Allen, whom he loved, albeit in his own well-hidden way, more than life itself.

Only after he had killed the enemy knight, returned with Piers and reported to the baron, had he time to think again—and found that he still could not. It had been almost too easy to prevail in the combat, for William had been told so many times that sparring counted for nothing when it came to true battle. But a real man had fallen almost as easily as a straw practice dummy. He had done what he had to do, and triumphed. William thought distantly of the fact that he had taken a life, the first time he had ever done so. It did not move him, for all that he had dreaded this inevitable duty for so long. Perhaps it was as his father had told him as a boy; he was a natural knight, destined for those duties just as he was born to them.

And otherwise he should be glad. It seemed that Piers might live if the fates were kind and rot did not develop. Apparently he was already demanding wine and boasting of his brush with death. His account of the engagement bore little relation to the truth, but neither of his companions was inclined to correct him, even if their company had been welcomed, which it was not. However, he and Allen had received more praise for his rescue than criticism for allowing him to come to harm in the first place, and many of the old troops saw their small triumph as a fortunate omen. But the more William thought about it the less important such considerations seemed.

William's thoughts veered away into foggy dissolution. His duplicate mare had vanished away within an hour of being returned to the horse-line, much to his squire's confusion. The lad was relieved, but further confused, by William's mild response to the loss. Then there were Allen's piercing glances and increasingly ominous silence. He wanted his old friend's company as a welcome salve to his discomfort, but the longer he stayed the closer Allen came to asking about his preoccupations. It was miraculous that Allen had stayed mute on the matter so long.

William sighed and bowed his head. His eyes drooped closed and drowned him in proper darkness. He regretted these small actions even as they were made. They would give Allen the opening he had been awaiting all evening. He heard Allen stand quietly and felt a hand upon his shoulder. His respite, it seemed, was at an end.

"What is wrong, William, what have you done?"

William did not know what Allen meant exactly, or what he had observed to produce this concern. He had been there, of course, and might have seen anything. Was it merely Wiliam's own behavior, or had he seen something in the woods when the spirit came in horse-form to aid him? It must have been a good spirit surely to act so, an angel even? His heart did not think so. He looked up, sideways from his folded arms to where Allen stood leaning over him, his eyes glinting in the dim light. What he saw froze him in horror. Above Allen's head floated a diaphanous form, gray as spider webs and shimmering and glowing faintly. It looked like a small human skull wreathed in a pair of black-feathered wings and it was not static like a painting but even as he watched it began, feebly, to move.

William knew then that he was going mad, and how can one avoid that fall once it had begun? William did not want to credit what his eyes were showing him of late, but there was no way to live whilst disbelieving them. He stood and backed away from his old friend and the apparition that still attended him. Allen, in immediate concern, stepped towards him with his hands outstretched and beseeching. The horrible image followed, suspended eerily above his head. The phantom skull seemed to leer and grin at William, observing his reaction with its shadowed socket-eyes. It seemed to see him, and to regard him with a fixed and focused interest.

It was more than William's tenuous rationality could survive; he burst out of the tent and ran into the dark camp. It was late and most of the fires had been banked for the night, leaving little more than clouded stars and smoldering ashes to see by. William swore and stumbled over tent lines as he fled, drawing curses from those within. He passed a servant between the tents, which seemed normal, then a squire who bore above his head the same ominous winged-skull sigil. He saw several more so marked before he left the camp and staggered into the deep-grassed hills. If Allen had even tried to follow him, he would have been swiftly left behind—terror leant William wings.

William had read of witchcraft and demons, yet he had thought, like most men, to live his whole life without being directly or explicitly touched by such things, but now he felt the clammy fingers of evil closing around him. Like most, he sometimes even doubted that such things were real rather than fodder for sermons and parables for the instruction of wayward children.

Now he believed. He ran blindly, the deep dried stalks of brush and grass breaking across his shins. The branches of the low brambles clawed at him in passing; and he ran his hardest—as if damnation was a thing that could be thus avoided. He would have run to the end of the world and beyond, had he the strength. But it was vain hope that this was a peril that might be out-distanced.

His foot slammed into a depression, some hoof-pock or rabbit hole hidden in the grass, and he fell...and was caught. He froze then, helpless in fear. He became aware that his eyes were closed, and left them so. He was on his knees, pressed against the chest of a form, likewise positioned. The other's hands were flat and cool against his back, the body clad in some soft woven cloth that brushed softly against his cheek, and the arms that held him were strong and firm. There had been nobody around him as he ran, but on falling he was instantly embraced.

William briefly entertained the fantasy that it could somehow be Allen who held him, as he secretly wished he could be held. He would have been content even with any ordinary stranger, but such commonplace explanations were not tenable. The true answer awaited him if only he could muster the courage to open his eyes. It took a long moment, a very long moment, for him to do so.

He pushed backwards slowly and beheld a spotless white shirt, its lace trimmed collar tossing gently in the breeze that passed over the surface of the hill they occupied. Above it all, there was a pale-skinned face, distinguished by darkly beautiful features and an expression of superior amusement. It was the face of an icon, of a graven angel crowned with flyaway hair, and that impression was only strengthened by what William saw next. Behind that form there rose a pair of glossy black wings, almost imperceptible in the darkness apart from a languid movement that saw them rise and fall slowly, the feathers ruffling and shifting across their surfaces. There was something almost too real about those feathers, more like that of a giant crow that any icon's even, snowy rows of quills.

William crawled backwards and was released by this obliging apparition. He scrambled to his feet and the creature opposite stood smoothly to face him, offering nothing more threatening than an inquiring look and a steadying hand. William stared at him; even in the darkness each feature was clear, as if the strange angel's form was imbued with subtle blue-tinged light. Nothing in the world would have provoked William to speak first, but the obligation to do so was quickly lifted from him.

"You do not seem grateful for the gift of foresight that I have given you," the creature said in the warm tones of a familiar and chiding friend.

"*You* gave me?" William's lips stumbled gracelessly over the repetition.

"I did." The being caressed his cheek with careless affection, like a man stroking a favored pet. Then he stepped back to survey William, crossing his arms and tilting his head quizzically. "It is a rare gift, not lightly given."

William thought immediately of Allen, the first he had seen marked by the evil visions. He wondered if that same form floated over his own head although he forced himself not to attempt to see.

"What am I foreseeing then? What will befall Allen?" His concern forced past his fear and made him ask.

"The battle tomorrow will take him, of course, unless you save him. It is the death's head you see, and you will see far more in the fullness of time."

This was the devil, then, or a demon so high as to make no difference. No good could ever come of meeting an entity such as this. There was no purpose pure enough to enter into a pact with a being such as this and nothing to be gained from any act but turning now and fleeing its company. But that was not what he did.

Death hung over one whom he loved as a brother, what man could turn away from even the most hopeless of hopes? William knew himself to be a pawn of forces that made the baron nothing more than a laughable buffoon. All the concerns that had ruled his life—to hold the land, to be a knight, to somehow be a proper husband to his straying wife—suddenly seemed unimportant.

"Take me in his place," William said, serene in the knowledge that his wife and her coming child would be adequately supported by the lands he left them, and quite sure the world could more easily support his loss than that of golden Allen.

The beautiful creature before him merely laughed, a sound as high and sweet as copper bells chiming. "Oh, you, my dear William, are already damned. I am Ahriman and you are my creature. But to save your foster brother you could offer me...the child."

"The child?"

"The child your wife bears, to be mine immediately. She shall survive its loss, and you shall have an heir of your own body in due course. It should be a most agreeable solution to all," Ahriman purred.

"The child, the child is an innocent..."

"Of course, or he would be already mine. He is a most innocent bastard, but ask yourself this. Who is more deserving of your consideration, the unborn that knows not even that he has life, or your brother? For it must be at the very least one or the other."

William moaned, in fear and anguish, fixed in place by Ahriman's glittering ebon eyes. How was he the devil's already, how had he damned himself? William knew himself to be no saint but he had never before this day killed a man nor committed any cardinal sin. He had striven towards virtue all of his life, even denying the unnatural urges he felt towards other men because the scripture proscribed such acts. It hardly mattered, for he knew what he would do next would be enough to send him to hell even had he not already deserved it. At that moment he did not even feel the need to agonize over the decision. The answer, painful as it was, arose immediately and unbidden from deep within his unworthy heart. He was damned already and made a choice the damned man might blithely make.

"The babe," he whispered. "Take the babe."

With a slight murmur of the changing wind, Ahriman vanished softly away, leaving William cowering amongst the rank weeds of the hillside with an aching hole in his heart. He waited, frozen, for some time—but he was now alone. Alone but for his decision, his memory and his guilt. It would be merciful to die upon the spot rather than to live with the decision he had made. For life from this moment on could never be joyful, could never be anything other than a brief burden with everlasting damnation stretching beyond. What he had done to Margaret placed their betrothal beyond any rescue; there would never be anything he could do to compensate for the murder of her child. That it was not his, was no excuse.

William wondered if he was an evil man. After all, no man would easily think himself evil, or seek to embrace such a state. Surely it must come to any who ended up there in this way, ill chance and harsh dilemmas—choices made quickly and for selfish ends. He felt tears of self-pity gather in his eyes and harshly scrubbed them away. He deserved no pity even from himself. He had abetted in the murder of an innocent to save a friend; he had dealt with the devil. There was no going back now.

The promontory he stood upon was bare and almost total silence prevailed; a slight whisper of wind, a dull chink of metal from the camp, the distant hoot of an owl. The everyday world trundled on beyond the numb pall that covered William's senses. The best he could hope for now was to not drag down others with him. He would speak of this night to no man. None would know his guilt and none would share it.

What have I done? he wondered then spoke quietly to himself, knowing that his life would never be the same. "In either case, 'tis done."

He wrapped his arms around him and, lacking any other course of action, began to retrace his path back to the friend who would never know who saved him, or at what price.

Chapter Five

Allen was pleased that William agreed to use his spare mount for the battle, by that and nothing else. William had stormed out like a lunatic last night, stayed out 'til the early hours, returned morose and silent. Then he spent the whole night upon the ground with a blanket wrapped around him, despite any insistence Allen made that he should share or even take the bed himself. Now Will greeted this treacherous dawn looking wan and sleepless.

Will looked haunted; Allen felt deeply worried. It was a poor state in which to face any fight, let alone a pitched contest against seasoned knights. If Allen's self-serving summons proved a death sentence for his less experienced foster brother, he knew he would never forgive himself. In fact he had done little over the last few hours since sunrise but berate himself for ever sending that missive. Yes, he wanted William's company but he had thought to keep his more callow friend back from the heart of the battle and ensure his safety. Now he could tell that William would not be so backward or so biddable as to allow that. If Allen had given it a moment's thought, he should have known that, even were it not for the dark currents the last few days had stirred up.

Their well-acquainted steeds stood side by side at the base of the great sweeping meadow. Allen looked frequently to William, who stared stonily ahead. Granted, 'Black' Will had never been a bon vivant, but there had always been a warmth to him, a side he let Allen see if no one else. Now, strikingly and suddenly, it was gone. Under normal circumstances Allen might have seen it as nothing more than nerves, understandable on the threshold of his first battle. But Allen had seen William so coolly dispatch his opponent the previous day, and seen the wild look in his eyes when he dashed from the pavilion last night without a word of explanation for his moods. And...the other matter. It was strange...beyond strange, but this was not the time to be mentioning it.

Allen was, as ever, inclined to give William the benefit of the doubt but these last few days were beginning to strain both his nerves and his indulgence. If only there was some useful priest to confide in, but the baron's chaplain looked like a sanctimonious prig from a distance and Allen was not inclined to make his acquaintance let alone seek his advice.

Some of the men around them prayed as they stood, others were grimly silent, fidgeted, or chattered to their comrades. Allen mused that he must be one of the few along the line whose mind was not upon the impending battle. The wait might be long or short, but the danger after the charge would be very real. Battle was slaughter, and most here were old enough to know it. Allen never suffered much during the interminable wait.

If the imminent possibility of death had any effect at all it was to make Allen rather regret that he'd never pressed his luck with William. Life was, after all, wont to be short, especially for those who took up arms. He ventured as far as to reach over and pat William's shoulder reassuringly. William glanced up at him and gave a terse smile that stopped well short of his eyes, a token gesture. Allen wondered if he should speak. Many a man might divulge matters in this sort of moment that he would otherwise take to his grave. As witness Allen's own sudden urge, which was to tell William he loved him. A foolish thing, but there it was. He was almost ready to say it and the consequences be damned...

Just at that moment, the horns sounded their first burst. All about, reins were taken up and horses shifted their feet, anticipating action. A murmur of predictable comments was passed.

"Here we go, at last."

Banners that had been drooping were raised high by eager hands: Hambly's boar rampant on azure, and many a personal sigil. Those of more modest provision made do with a painted shield. Allen's eyes dropped to his own shield, its leather cover painted with a simple blue chevron and yellow scallops in a line. It was not a particularly brave symbol to fight for, a stripe and some shells; it represented an old and distinguished family to be sure but he was never likely to be more than a barren cul-de-sac of the Cormerat bloodline. He was a convenient way to satisfy the family's obligation to serve the king, and those of his nobles he lent his favors to.

His well-worn contemplation was cut short. The second horn blast sent them forth in the grim chaos of the charge. Allen was in no haste to be first, yet William spurred ahead, as if hurrying to his death, and Allen did his best to go after. The still air became heavy with the harsh breaths and hoof-falls of horses; some of the men shouted their defiance to bolster their own courage. In the distance, a faint compliment to these sounds swelled up as the broken horizon resolved itself into their opponents, neighbors turned enemy by the vagaries of noblemen's intrigues.

Both forces had elected to charge almost at the same moment, the heavy horses pushing their great hooves deep into the moist sod. It was not the swiftest of engagements, but was all the more horrible for its inexorable sloth. As soon as the foremost met, the battle dissolved into tempests of isolated acts of violence. The big horses slowed before meeting, searching for a gap as their riders sought the advantage. Weapons resounded as they struck at metal armor and cut at wooden shields with heavy thuds. These sound defenses meant that many a blow was struck without an answering cry of pain. Some men just rained down as many heavy blows as they could muster; others used some skill to hold them 'til they had a chance of falling true and upon a weakness. Allen was more of that kind and respected for it. Those who knew his heraldry treated him with caution and spurred their horses to try and approach him from his offside, or even pass him over for easier prey.

Allen did not chase these cowards down. He kicked his baulking mare and drove her forward, striving to keep William in sight. But it would have been easier to pursue a wraith, for Will became a will 'o the wisp, darting swiftly amidst the brawl striking here and there where the blows counted the most. William was showing an uncanny instinct for battle and within a short spell of time many of Hambly's men had cause to be grateful for his intercession. Allen saw him in snatches harrying the enemy and moving swiftly. He made few decisive blows but prevented the enemy knights in their attacks. Allen turned his head, craning for another glimpse of William amidst the melee. He had thought to try and guard this novice combatant but could hardly even keep him in view. It seemed that for all Allen's skills it might be William who featured in more grateful tales when evening came.

The flat of a sword glanced off Allen's bracer, and a shiver of weakness ran up his arm. It forced him to turn his mind entirely to the preservation of his own life. His mare answered his knee-signals as well as if she were on the practice field. She wheeled so that Allen might meet his opponent with his shield arm. This knight had the grizzled beard of a seasoned campaigner and at his back a younger version, his son no doubt, was sawing his reins to try and flank him. Allen put honor a little to the side, as a man does when he'd rather not die.

Allen drove his sword into the older man's steed. His blade went deep in its flank and the horse squealed and bucked so hard that he was hard-pressed to pull his weapon free. The older man was made awkward by his armor and fell heavily to the ground. His son rode to shield him from further attack. Allen preferred this foe, young and brash with a half-trained mount. He let his mare pick her own path; she knew well that he wanted to be close and danced within arm's reach. The young man's foolish stallion snorted and reared; a fiery beast is truly the worst thing in battle. The man flailed his arm, exposing the vulnerable armpit. It was the ability to see these moments, and the speed to act upon them, that made the difference between a nobleman in shiny armor and a useful knight.

Allen slid his blade in smoothly, feeling it grate on the man's ribs. He twisted his hand slightly and brought his blade back, blooded. He did not even pause to watch his opponent fall. The act of killing did not bother Allen overly; acts in the press of battle were understood as just a duty of the post. You might toast a man at his wedding one day and slay him the next if the tides of earthy power drew a line of battle between him and you. And when the necessity passed, grudges were not held, for yesterday's enemy may be tomorrow's ally against some other common foe.

Some feet away, another of Hambly's followers was hard-pressed by one of the earl's knights and a pike man on foot. Allen spurred towards him, too late to save him, and inherited his foes. Thus engaged, he forgot Will and his recklessness awhile, or at least it was not foremost on his mind. He wielded his heavy sword like a scythe, cutting down any man who rose up before him or beating them aside. His arm grew weary with the work and he could feel his horse trembling beneath him, her sides streaked with sweat and lather. The edges of his armor chafed his skin with each movement and he struggled to maintain his speed and vigilance. His eyes and mind saw his chances as they came and he forced his body to exploit them, sure in the knowledge that one day it would not answer.

Time wore on as Allen spurred from fight to fight, as the knots and flurries of combatants drifted farther apart amidst the rolling terrain. He was struggling to keep his life and cost at least two men theirs and few others some serious wounds. He did not strain to see who fell and who stayed fallen, not being the type of man to keep a tally to boast about. Those he unhorsed he left, if they were wise and fled afoot they might live and with his blessing. It was more important to face down those still on their mounts than bother with those at the level of their feathered fetlocks. Still, William's plight intruded upon his thoughts from time to time, for all that not even a glimpse of him presented itself to Allen's acute eye.

His mare stumbled and Allen was caught unawares, thrown over her neck and to the ground. He stopped himself from grasping at the reins, she was a well-mannered horse and keeping hold of his weapons was more important. The mare redeemed herself by striking out as she had been trained, knocking back a yeoman who sought to take advantage of Allen's misfortune. Allen staggered to his feet, gasping to force air back into his winded lungs. He dropped his shield; it had cracked in the fall and was too long to use afoot. He took his sword in both hands and turned towards the shadow that he knew would be the yeoman as soon as he could focus his eyes upon it. He did not wait that long to act. In a desperate lunge, he plunged his blade forward whilst his foe was still nonplussed, piercing straight through his inadequate leather armor.

The man staggered back and fell, gasping. There was no doubt he was mortally wounded—blood flowed from his mouth and his eyes held the glassy realization of his impending demise. Knowing no further attack would come; Allen looked around but saw nothing save a fleeing knight and some signs of more distant action. He stepped forward to deliver a mercy blow only to see that it was no longer needed. The man lay on his back, a useless piece of clay now that the spirit had fled. It was ridiculous how a length of steel could so easily undo that miraculous work that was a man.

It was strange, he considered, how the old sagas and new romances depicted battles as long duels with many sleights and passes. More often it was like this, one or a few blows might be exchanged before you were pulled apart by the movements of the field, or as sometimes happened, a mortal blow was delivered. More often it was like wolves chasing a stag. If it ran it often outpaced them, if it stood it often held them off. It took a good wolf and an unlucky stag for nature to show its cruelest face. One had to react quickly and seize the advantage when it came, beyond that it was simply a matter of chance or destiny. Allen crossed himself at the thought and gave thanks for his own luck holding.

Allen's mare came to his hand, though an arrow stub projected from her haunch. Allen patted her bowed neck gently. He could hear the horns now, blowing a retreat and it seemed to him they might have been sounding for some time. They were the horns from the earl's camp, but if one side disengaged, the other could do little but harry them to the edge of the field of battle. It was a matter of highest honor that the fighting happened only where and when both sides consented. For how could God favor the righteous if the contest was not properly delineated? Allen shook his head at the tenor of his own thoughts, dancing dangerously close to agnosticism. Many might follow rules and have faith, but battles were odd creatures and seemed to fall the way of those who could call on more and better men, regardless of the worthiness of the cause. Indeed, Allen knew the facts of the current engagement and saw no reason for God to prefer the baron's greed over the earl's self-defense.

"I hope to God this fight is done," he said to his forlorn horse.

It was noon, perhaps, and he could hear no further clash of arms. Both sides drew apart, ahorse or afoot, and began to trek back to their own camps, pausing here and there to aid the wounded or examine the dead. Carrion birds had started to alight upon the supine shapes of fallen men and beasts. The lull might still prove to be brief, if the earl's forces rallied and charged again. He made for the safety of the baron's camp, knowing he should not lag behind to lead his injured mare, but unwilling to desert such a valuable and faithful beast. She followed his lead gamely but with one hind leg raised and her head bobbing deep with each lurching step. He inspected every fallen man he passed but each was either of the enemy or beyond help. One of the earl's men moaned in fear at the sight of him; a young man with both arms shattered and useless either by the blow of an axe or mace, or perhaps the hooves of horses once he had fallen.

"Don't worry," Allen said in passing. "We're done, for now, and your people will be looking for you. Call out, so they can find you."

On a slight rise, Allen glanced around. He could see youthful squires and servants coming now to retrieve the wounded, and the bodies of the dead. Servants from both sides could be distinguished by their bright livery – their presence on the field signaling that the battle was in fact over until the morrow at least. Allen's own manservant, Yarrow, waited at his pavilion as instructed. Allen had more faith in his ability to return than his man's ability to find him amidst the aftermath of combat.

Of William, there was no sign. Had he another mount to use, Allen would have ridden out immediately in search. He stood uncertainly at the flap of his great tent. Yarrow and his young son drew him inside and stripped his armor wordlessly from him. Once its weight was lifted, his body felt as light as a ghost, yet he was still exhausted. His arms and thighs trembled and he felt horribly cold as his drenched undergarments were stripped away. He turned away the robe that Yarrow offered and called for his clothes.

He went about the camp until he was sure Will did not lie with either the wounded or the dead. He gave serious thought to going afoot back to the field of battle, but it was a long and treacherous way with no surety of there being any point to it. The baron's men would not leave any man to lie upon the field, he could rely on that. He went back to doctor his poor nag, with a crease of worry lodged on his temple. Dread settled over him and the harsh cries of crows made a fitting accompaniment.

Chapter Six

William had never raised his sword in anger before the previous day, although he had sparred often enough on the practice ground. He wondered at the ease with which he took to war. He was well prepared to look something of a fool, so long as his effort and intent were marked—yet that prospect seemed unlikely to him now. He felt no particular fear as the hour of combat neared. In the context of his other fears, mere death seemed less awful for all that he did not court it. He could view his impending peril with the kind of pragmatism that he imagined the older men acquired.

When the horns resounded across the low hills of the chosen ground, William spurred his borrowed horse and tried to leave Allen far behind. William knew the taint of the devil was upon him and whether he lived or died, it was better he stayed well away from any man he wished well. The misty apparitions still dotted the field; floating over the heads of men here and there, the death's heads leered. Allen, however, no longer seemed to be amongst the doomed. William wondered if that grisly spectacle floated above his own head, blocked from view by the padded brow of his simple dish-shaped helm. He did not try to look; he did not want to know.

Now that the charge had come, William simply did whatever seemed best to do. It was almost liberating to have a straightforward duty to perform, no matter how perilous. He wove through the other horses and crashed through the forefront of the enemy lines, striking at those who fought on the earl's side. He did not stand his ground but kept moving as best as he could, seeking out any of the baron's forces that were hard-pressed and drawing off some who harried them. His sword seemed to find its own way to where it was best needed, drawing his body behind it. The less he thought about his actions the more smoothly and aptly they flowed. Perhaps this ease of killing was just part of the hidden taint within him, the darkness that had drawn the devil to him.

He knew that he was holding his own, although his shield arm was becoming heavy. It was hard to tell how many of his blows fell true in the maelstrom of the action where attention must be paid to whomever drew close rather than following any one enemy or single exchange. He forged through the heart of the conflict, trusting fate to do as she saw fit and darting left and right to force men apart, strike where they were weak or distract their aim from an unwary or trapped target. Not a few of his comrades had cause to be thankful for his intervention; William was swift and held his own even if it was often those with a stronger arm who drove home the deathblow. He dared imagine that he was playing his part on the baron's behalf. He dared hope some of the men might speak well of him when the fight was over. Certainly he had not held back and only the hardened steel breastplate left to him by his father had saved him from being run through on several occasions. An arrow bounced from his small helm, making him wonder if he would have been wiser to wear his great helmet even though it hampered his sight and movement. With time he pushed through into a sparser area where the ground was rough and deeply grassed, making the horse slow, unsure of her ground.

The baron's forces were starting to turn the battle and the press of horses was easing as word passed amongst their enemy to disengage, although no horns had yet been blown for full retreat. Allen had told him that the first day of battle was often short and less intense than those that would follow. They were feeling each other out and bearing news back to the commanders.

William went with a group of knights that chased after their opponents as they withdrew. Blows crashed off his raised shield as he galloped by their side, ringing coppery pain down his exhausted muscles. His mare was less than game to give more speed, whereas those who saw they were homeward bound found new vigor to return to their well deserved rest and comforts. William dug in his heels and insisted on greater effort, which, grudgingly, she gave. He was on the last of his strength also, but meant to use it well.

William was one of the last to give up that chase. He wheeled upon the brow of a small rise. Clusters of knights from each side were congregating; men found their particular friends and stuck by them now that the fight was winding down and men were withdrawing. Fights were still breaking out as these groups met each other upon the field. In the eddies of the ongoing conflict, a group of riders moving with fixed purpose was immediately clear to the eye. William saw that four knights riding abreast were turning towards him.

He could swear he even heard one say, "Finally, there 'tis. The white lady."

It sent a chill through his bones, for the white lady was his own device, painted on his scarred leather shield-cover and sewn upon his saddlecloth. The knights fixed their gazes on

William's shield and spurred towards him specifically. They seemed to be close comrades, wheeling almost as one and with parade-ground procession to thunder towards him. William could only imagine he had struck some particular friend of theirs in the melee, and they sought to even the score before the horns sealed that quarrel forever into the past. He noticed that they all wore only the earl's heraldry and not their own, men of Serle's own household, taking their stipend from his hand. They turned from their withdrawal to pursue him and William saw no valor in standing to be slaughtered by them, he sawed his mare's bridle to turn her sharply aside.

William knew he could not effectively fight against such odds, whatever their reason for singling him out. He kicked his horse down into the dell and knew he was not mistaken when all of them pursued him with fixed intent and some vigor. One was on a swift young mare who took the bit between her teeth and gained upon him rapidly. He marked the look in the leading man's eyes—grimly determined, not marked with any intense emotion. Not a grudge then, though no other explanation occurred to him.

William had hoped to circle back towards his own camp but they veered in to cut off that escape and herd him towards the far side of the field. He spurred hard and shouted his mare on. He hoped to outpace them and dart around before them. He ceased straining to watch them and bent over his horse's neck. He made for the far left of the field for if he couldn't get around them he could see the trees. Surely they would not pursue him beyond the agreed edge of the field? And well, if they did he still might lose them under that cover. He focused on speed, on urging his flagging mount to greater effort.

A resounding blow upon his back caught him entirely by surprise and knocked him from the saddle; the ground rushed up to meet him and he hit hard under the full, entangled weight of all his armor. William stumbled to his feet as quickly as he could, knowing he was closely pursued, and looked desperately about. His flight had taken him some distance clear of the battle. Allen's mare might well have returned for her proper master, but on this occasion she rabbit-hopped twice, gave him a quick, guilty glance and bolted. William cursed his luck and turned to face his fate, whatever it might be.

Two of the knights saw him unhorsed and turned aside, leaving the other two to deal with him. One of those who went back to the center of the field was the one with the swift mare. William saw him swing his poleax back into attack position, grinning at his success.

"That should make it easy enough for you, Frank," he called back.

William could feel his plate pressing into his shoulder now, pounded in by the impact of that weapon. He tried to ignore the pain of it for there was no time to be fiddling with or removing his armor.

William hefted his sword, his gaze darting between the two that remained. They were both grim-faced men in middle age, one with a long brindle beard and another gaunt-faced man with shrewd, squinting eyes. It was this one who hung back as if he were far more used to giving orders than carrying them out.

"We'll have him for Festrigan," that one said. "Alive by preference but dead if he insists."

The bearded one raised a large mace, kicking his stocky gelding forward. William scuttled aside from the blow which fell heavy but slow. He could see Allen's gelding still running some distance off and not likely to look back before she was back on the horse-line with a bucket of oats and a warm blanket. There was nothing near at hand but a damp, grassy hillside and these two men. He could not even hope to run, as his attacker wheeled his horse to come at him again. Life had suddenly narrowed down to a single rather hopeless option, defend himself as best he could and hope to get away hale enough to walk back to his side of the lines. He wondered what on earth they would want with him alive, or at all. His only advantage was that the bearded man was well-armored and was more encumbered by it.

William steeled himself to fight and to strike where he could. Time and again he dodged the mace, trying to sidle back the way he had come but making little headway. His shield arm ached and his breath came in harsh fearful gasps as he darted this way and that each time the heavy hooves and hand wheeled at him again. Excruciating minutes passed. The disengagements of the two forces was not going cleanly, William could hear curses and the ringing tones of weapons clashing. He prayed that chance might bring other men from the baron's side to his small corner of the field; he could not hope to prevail alone.

"Take me alive, when your comrades are still fighting!" William yelled. "How can I be so important?"

His attacker merely smiled and pressed forward again. William's foot stuck in the sucking mud as he tried to dodge away and he had to raise his shield to block the mace. It fell, as heavy as the hand of God, and split the shield vertically from top to bottom. William threw it aside and took his sword in both hands as he wrenched his foot free. His whole arm ached, right down his spine and his ankle was jagged with sharp pains as he tried to put his weight upon it. So now he was all but defenseless, slow and dog-tired. It was only a matter of time before they wore him down.

For a moment he wondered whether he should yield. He would take no more part in the fighting and only inconvenience the baron further rather than aid him. But on top of that, if the baron would not ransom him, he might be trapped long in hostile hands with Margaret and his estates left in difficult circumstances. Besides all that, what else would any knight of honor do but fight until he could fight no more? He raised his sword and sighted down the blade at the broad-shouldered knight who watched him dispassionately like a hunter might regard its prey.

The bearded one dismounted and approached on foot, perhaps as a gesture to fair play—or just because his vantage from horseback did not favor his accuracy. William saw that the man was about his own height but almost twice as broad and approaching with the cool confidence of one well used to warfare. William waved his own, suddenly puny-seeming, blade and made a defensive stance.

"Give it up, lad; come with us quietly and you'll live. There's nothing to be gained by making it difficult."

William made no reply, but tightened his grip and lunged with the long blade ahead of him. His opponent stopped and swung his mace one more time. William dropped under the blow but his own blade just skated off the curved profile of the man's armored breastplate. He saw an opening, but stepping to the side, his ankle failed him and he went down on one knee. He survived the moment unharmed only because his opponent chose that moment to toss aside his mace and draw his own sword.

"Having to take the pup seriously, are you?" said new voice.

The forces were finally drawing apart and a hush began to descend. Unfortunately, it seemed that William was on the wrong side of the lines and every passing moment made it even less likely that anybody would be coming to his aid. Two armed horsemen bearing the earl's sigil joined the audience, treating William's situation as something of an entertainment.

"We'll have him alive," the big man said as he gave his sword a few practice passes. "Old Festrigan wants him."

William had little left in him to fight with, but pointless anger at the way they dismissed him with jokes, and he rode the wave of it. He staggered to his feet and drove his blade up at a weakness in the armor. He was pleased to make the man stagger back and raise his shield. William took three measured steps as he struck with all of his waning strength, again and again, forcing his advantage and leaving no gap for a riposte. He was satisfied to see the big man continue to back away at the force of his barrage. He may not be winning this fight but he would see it through with some honor. He saw a glint of skin as the man's cloak caught under his foot and the pressure of it displaced his shoulder plate. He drove the blow forward with a cry, cut short. He had just enough time to decide that the devil does not, after all, look after his own before all sense fled.

Samuel Cole handed Frank back his discarded mace. Frank took it in one broad hand whilst the other felt his neck, where the very tip of the young knight's sword had scratched him. It would have done more if the force had not been knocked out of the blow by his old friend's intervention.

"Reckon the lad might've had you," Sam said.

"Reckon he might," Frank agreed ruefully. "He's got quite good form for a green 'un. A good helmet too I reckon, looks like he's still alive." He kicked the young man over onto his back with one booted foot and watched closely to ensure he was not feigning his senseless state. "To be fair I was hampered by trying to keep him alive and he, it seems, had no such qualms."

Frank was mindful of not looking too good in that last exchange, and he the earl's champion...well. It was youth no doubt; the younger men kept their strength better throughout the battle even if they were built thin like this one. There was no cause to take his embarrassment out on the poor lad now that he had the better of him. He bent to strip off the young knight's armor, as it would make him easier to carry.

"Why do you think old Festrigan wants him?" he asked idly as he looked down at the still face of the senseless knight.

The young man looked no more than twenty and five years, Frank had two sons and a daughter all older than that. He had no hesitation in doing what the earl wanted, but he trusted the old scholar a good deal less. Festrigan had the look of a driven man and not one to cross if it could be avoided. Frank shrugged, it was simply not his part to question his betters' ways no matter how strange they became.

It was old Rodger who answered. "They say Ol' Festy thinks this un's a witch of some sort," he said in an uncommitted voice.

They both know that the earl's advisor was a devout man and a scholar of note—but he did hold some undeniably peculiar ideas. Frank just shrugged and hefted the not-quite-so dead weight of the young man over his shoulder.

Chapter Seven

Margaret lay upon the couch in her husband's chamber. She stood and roamed about his empty rooms, searching for some way to understand the strange cold place her life had become. The furniture, of course, told her nothing. The room was chilly and stale and both aspects somehow symbolic of their marriage, that and the fact that this room was unfamiliar to her eyes. William had given her a dedicated suite of rooms, and they met only in the common living spaces rather than in either private chamber.

She had demanded the key to these locked doors from Shandrick, and it had taken her a good long while to convince him to hand them over. Shandrick was a dedicated man, faithful to the estate more than anything else, but also to William. But Margaret suspected she had Shandrick's sympathy, and that she would need it.

"We are married, one person, his rooms are mine also— or should be," she had told him.

Should be, indeed. But Shandrick was a man who believed in essential truths like this, willing to put more weight on the golden ideal than the obvious reality. Margaret manipulated him almost unconsciously. Being raised in the area of the court reserved for mistresses should have prepared her to wind any man around her little finger. William, in particular, should have been no challenge; a man naive in as many ways as he was educated. But it was just as her mother had warned her—it is when you need your wiles the most that a man becomes the most opaque. Mother put that down to love, but Margaret was more inclined to blame the perversity of God.

She did not know that she *loved* William; although she did not doubt that she could, if only her regard might be returned. He was an honest enough man, and not ugly. Margaret was a pragmatic woman and did not require fairy tales and breathless infatuation at first sight; she thought William might suit her well enough, if he cared to.

A year ago she had lived in the petty court, daughter of one of the king's former mistresses and subtly courted as potentially his bastard daughter. She had never been bothered too much because a bastard child was of interest only if the king favored them, and Harild had never so much as looked her way with undue interest. Now she was subject to another man whom she rarely saw and who did not esteem her. It was a most dispiriting pattern in her life. Perhaps that is why the child had begun to dominate her thoughts. This child and any other she might subsequently have would change the very center of her life, perhaps for the better. The idea of a family began to galvanize her thoughts, and every obstacle in her way began to seem like an opponent worth defeating.

But that morning she had begun to bleed. Her maid Clarisse had known the cause immediately but Margaret had denied it for hours. A little blood was not so unusual for a pregnant woman to pass, she said. Yet this was more than a little and by noon the child...the promise of a child, had been lost. It was not such an uncommon misfortune and she supposed she should be quietly pleased, under the circumstances. Instead she felt a peculiarly dislocated kind of grief. The child had not been asked for and hardly convenient, but she had become used to the idea of it.

A moment of frustration, a celebration fair in a village rife with pagan ritual and hard cider, a chance meeting with one of workers who came down through the lowlands to bring in the harvest. By the time she knew for sure that a child had resulted, the man responsible was nothing but a nameless memory. If she had been a single girl, she would have raised her "child of the fair" as many did, without shame. But she was no such thing, and the guilt wore heavy on her.

She had begun to see a life with the child however, a girl preferably. William would soften to her and perhaps a son and heir would follow. She would ask a few particular friends to join her at the Tor and build a household, and a life.

It was still only a dream, a beginning of a dream—perhaps more doomed even than the child. She stood and wandered about the room, laying her hands upon the well-worn possessions that lay scattered around. Pens lay trimmed and ready upon William's desk, vellum unrolled and a gold stirrup weighed down a pile of correspondence. She lifted the top page from where it lay face down beneath that weight. Before even considering the propriety of the act, she read the first few lines written there.

"...Can only assume the king also doubts you and seeks to know your mind. He sends you a wife from his very household, perhaps from his own loins."

She had begun at the top of the second page, and turning and lifting the first she saw the full message of the unsigned letter. It warned that the Baron Hambly wished to seize the lands at White Lady Tor, and the king might easily be convinced to give his blessing. The informant's opinion was that in deciding whether to indulge the Baron Hambly in his plans the king had sent a spy into the household, the child of a favored mistress. The final speculation was the most damning. If William were killed, the whole estate would go to Margaret, to the care of her nearest male relative and as a woman of unclaimed paternity. The death of Margaret's husband would pass his lands in all honor to the king to keep or bestow as he willed. And one thing was certain; the king would always have a use even for such a small plum, to use as a reward or a goad in his labyrinthine plans.

It was all too plausible. Margaret knew herself to be no spy, to have never exchanged more than the briefest of pleasantries with the king, but otherwise the rest might well be true. The king was a conniver, he acted out of his duty to preserve and protect the lands of Ordran, but he acted callously at times. He did not concern himself too much with single men or women; everything was overshadowed by his concern for the stability of the realm. He might well have plans for the estate at the Tor, whether to gain leverage over Hambly or reward one of his own men. Harild would be capable of murder—most causal murder—if it served his ends.

And William had placed himself where his death would be considered ridiculously commonplace. Any untried knight upon a field of battle? He might be dead even now, and all her planning for naught. Margaret pressed her hands against her empty belly. There was not even an child to dissuade him, nor the rumor of one. William would not have spoken of the matter, regardless of his feelings, so early on the pregnancy. If she had the child, she could try and plead widowhood to keep the lands for herself....

She shook that selfish thought aside. William must live yet, or at least she would assume he was and act on his behalf. She would be a good wife for Sir William of White Lady Tor, whether he deserved it or not. Perhaps if she took strong steps to act her proper role, the rest would fall in place. Well, proper to the extent an opinionated bastard daughter of a mistress could ever be proper. Margaret smiled. Being meek had not won her husband 'round—now she would just be herself and see how he dealt with that.

She read the letter's lies over again, searching for truths and possibilities. She considered what allies she might call on, for herself or on her husband's behalf. They were few enough. Looking at those poisonous words again, she understood William's most extreme reticence. He suspected her of being a spy, and perhaps even an assassin. All of those times when he had seemed almost ready to speak to her, she wondered what he had meant to say. Perhaps it was these accusations that were poised on his lips, and she in her foolishness had supposed it might be the first protestations of love.

The marriage was at the king's decree and so rather hasty. She had hoped he was simply taking the time to court her belatedly, and perhaps the growing awkwardness has been partly her own doing in waiting for him to make his move, but giving little away herself. The ongoing silence had been poison between them; she should have had the sense to break it. If they had spoken of these matters, she could have told the truth. She had nothing to lose by it and a great deal to gain.

There was really very little that she could do. Propriety demanded restraint—that she would wait here for his return, no matter how uncertain that return was. Margaret was well used to waiting. She had endured a lifetime of waiting. In court, she had learned feminine crafts, weaving and sewing and embroidery with ribbons, bided her time, waiting for the king to arrange her marriage. All those pointless crafts that did little but wile away the days of a woman's life when nobody else had a use for her. When her engagement had finally occurred, she had been fairly pleased. As a women without title or dowry, she had expected no better than to be given thoughtlessly as a trophy to some aging courtier. Instead she found herself sent to a pleasant part of the land, to a man her own age and easy enough to look at. She had hoped to love him, and in time to be loved. How it had confounded her to discover he was impenetrably aloof, and all but mute in her presence.

She had to get to him before he came to any harm; she had to explain her innocence. She had gone from her mother's house to her husband's and she would do her best to protect his interests whether he appreciated it or not. Even given very little cause, Margaret felt an allegiance to William. He may not be a wise man but he had simple goals, to hold what he had. Even that did not seem for the purpose of his own aggrandizement but in the memory of the parents he still so openly mourned.

Margaret felt a determined ire rising up within her. She would go after William. Men did take their wives on campaign sometimes, it was not unheard of. Certainly where there were knights, there were always women of all types in attendance. And she would not trundle along with a dozen servants and wagonloads full of unnecessary trappings. She would go swiftly and as unencumbered as she could manage. She would take the letter and have the conversation they should have had when they first met, and certainly before they went down the narrow aisle of the local church together. Margaret was done with waiting, it well past time for her to act and to seize the moment for another may not come.

She had carried out many arguments with Shandrick, the old man was set in his ways, but this, no doubt, would be the fiercest. Tucking the spiteful letter in her bodice, she went to seek him out. It was uniquely liberating to know that after all these years of waiting, now she would act.

ക്കൈ

Ahriman watched the woman. She would be a pleasing part of the play. William had burned the letter, not being stupid enough to put his faith in locks. But it was simple matter to reproduce it and put it in her way. The matter of the battle had become too inevitable to bother observing so Ahriman had taken himself back to the wee castle on the Tor. Hambly would lose; William would be captured, but sweet little Margaret? Well, she still trembled on the cusp of a number of possible resolves and Ahriman did not know which of them he preferred.

William was one thing. He was a man of delicate moods but a straightforward mind and perhaps not too difficult to break, what was the sport in that? There were two people around him who were stronger, the knight Allen and his wife. If he could bring those two together, things became more complex. And Ahriman reveled in complexity, much more his element than evil or cruelty, although those were almost inevitably its results. If Ahriman was going to dabble in mortal lives, he would see to it that these mortals would deserve that attention. Margaret was living up to his expectations; he smiled and removed his invisible presence from the room in order to make a few other preparations.

He did not need to watch Margaret make her plans. She would argue for the sense of riding astride but the old man would prevail to the extent of a carriage. On the whole, the strength of her will and advantage of her rank would rule the day. It was only a light carriage and it would be Shandrick who drove it. If they met trouble on the road, one old man would be little defense. Margaret hardly considered the possibility of any obstacles and Shandrick was swept along in her wake.

Ahriman determined that they would not meet such trouble. In the interest of greater travails, this small one would be forestalled. He was looking forward to seeing how the next few days developed. For the first time, he wondered about the Regent's Bridle. He was not entirely sure he wanted to see it used. Despite what muttering priests and scholars might think, it was not demons that the Bridle held back, it was dragons. That strange artifact had been shaped by one of the last great human magicians, just before the last dragons of exile were slain a century ago. He rather missed the dragons but they were trouble on a different scale altogether.

So long as the Bridle was held by a descendent of Lukas, the worlds of men and dragons could be parted or joined by that person's will and folk could pass between them. It had been a number of years since it had been lost and Ahriman had no particular desire to see it back in mortal hands just yet. Once it was in the hands of a man, he would inevitably give it use. The dragons, well, they were beings that rivaled Ahriman's own powers and the magic they brought raised up great human mages. As much as the resulting chaos would be amusing, Ahriman was becoming used to being a power without effective opposition. Still, perhaps he should retain that option—vanity was not always to be indulged, even in himself.

Shandrick brought an extra pair of horses and tethered them to the rear of the carriage. He did not intend for them to pause for the night, but press on until they reached William, and to do that he would drive all night at speed. It made for a bumpy ride put Margaret clung to her seat and endured it.

Once they hit the highway, the ride became smoother and gradually she drifted into sleep.

In the depth of the night, she woke to find the carriage had stopped. Cautiously, she opened the door and stepped out onto the ground. She wished that she could have sat up on the driver's seat in the open air, but Shandrick would not hear of it. They were drawn up beside a wild and empty stretch of the highway. He was uncoupling the horses to exchange the teams in the hope that those who had run without burden would have strength now to spare. Margaret caught his eyes and nodded her head to the nearby shrubbery. Her bladder was fit to burst and little as he might like it, she was certainly going to have to step outside of his line of sight for a moment. It would be just her luck to find a band of brigands behind the thorn bushes.

Looking around cautiously, she lifted her skirts and crouched down on the damp ground. She attempted to urinate in absolute silence, embarrassed at being so near to Shandrick and his attentive ears. She wouldn't put it past him to come to check on her before she was finished. As she stood, she saw a glint of metal on the ground, right where she had squatted. She hesitated to look closer but curiosity gripped her. She nudged the object with the toes of her shoes, which concealed by her skirts were sensible boots rather than the dainty slippers that might be expected. The dirt fell away somewhat more. A more determined kick pushed it loose. She pulled a handkerchief from her sleeve and picked up what appeared to be a small statue. It seemed to be made from a fairly base metal, but it gleamed brightly and every graven detail was quite clear even in the darkness. It seemed to be some kind of mythical creature with scales and clawed talons but the creature wore on its head what appeared to be a bridle such as might be used on a common horse. She wiped its surfaces carefully; the whole figure was no larger the size of a clenched fist. She slipped it into her pocket and discarded the soiled handkerchief on the ground.

She was not sure what such an object was—it seemed rather too grotesque to be an ornament—nor how it came to by buried by the side of the road. But something drew her to keep it. Perhaps it was because it appeared to be a dragon, the symbol Harild had taken as his own device. Perhaps it was some joking elaboration that had broken from an ornate carriage? It seemed quite harmless to keep it.

Margaret returned to the carriage, to Shandrick's obvious relief. She paused before alighting.

"I am sorry to cause you such trouble," she said plainly.

"No," he said in a very different tone to that he had employed before. "I've been thinking on it, and remembering Will's dear mother. Better a woman be strong, and know her mind. Once I've shown I'll serve your interests, perhaps you'll tell me what it is you know."

Margaret climbed silently into the carriage, but she rather suspected that she would.

Chapter Eight

William lay still, feeling the ache in his bones. His whole back felt frozen, hurt and stiffened on a cold, hard floor. He was freezing, lying on what felt like bare stones and his head felt as fragile as an egg fallen from the nest. His natural caution bade him to stay still as he searched his mind for some hint, some clue, as to what had happened to him. He recalled the battle, and pulling on that thread he teased out the rest. He remembered his deal with Ahriman, forward to his last conscious moments. He remembered Allen's glance of concern, he remembered the last time he saw Margaret as she watched him leave the castle with a mask-like face, he remembered the devil on a starry hillside offering him an unwinnable dilemma. Despair dropped down onto him and stole any desire to do more than lie there and itemize his discomforts. Under the circumstances, he was only mildly curious as to where he was at the present moment, but sure the answer would be a grim one and so in no hurry to discover it. Perhaps he was never fit to be a knight, for it was in moments like these that a man with true courage revealed himself.

His one out-flung hand felt very slightly warm, as if sunshine fell upon it but only weakly. William's mind dwelled vacantly upon that simple sensation as a distraction from other less pleasant. A fly landed on his lips and without thought he jerked in disgust. Pain jolted through his head, and he felt the swaddling of a bandage about his brow. Finally his eyes opened to properly face the return of consciousness. He was in a small room, bare of any furniture except a plain bench seat made from large stone blocks without mortar, which stretched across the short end of the room. On the opposite wall there was a thick-beamed door braced with steel and pierced with a grill-covered window. The light from the small window above the bench splayed across the floor, and raising his eyes, William saw the sky covered with what looked like a bloody dusk.

He was not entirely on his own in this tiny room. No, not so fortunate. Right next to him were a pair of pale ankles clad in delicate sandals, and next to them the trailing edge of a pair of iridescent black wings. The figure's whole body was faintly translucent like a stained glass window made flesh, coloring but not obscuring William's view of the room beyond. He wondered for a moment whether the devil needed to wear shoes, or did so merely as some form of decoration.

Discomfort and light-headedness emboldened William. "Am I in hell then?" he asked.

Ahriman crouched by his side; his face was cast in a look of refined amusement.

"Is that any way to greet me? And I came here to give you a gift."

"Please don't," William said in all honesty. That last thing he needed in his life was more of the devil's gifts.

"I can give you a power, an ability. There are many interesting ways in which I can change a man, if I will it. Surely you would like that? I could show you how to drift out of the room like smoke. I could give you the ability to beguile any woman...or man, with your charm."

It was strange how talking to the devil was swiftly becoming ordinary. William supposed that if the devil was too outraged by his conduct he could blast him, send him directly to hell. The prospect did not seem particularly worse than continuing as he was, and that was enough to pierce his remaining anxiety. He was determined not to oblige his apparent master too easily. If the devil wanted him to escape then perhaps his best strategy was to stay. His best guess was that he was in the earl's dungeon, for whatever reason. And it seemed he could do nobody any harm if he stayed there for a while. It was a decision his body seconded, as it felt like he was hardly able to do any more than lie still.

"Where am I?" he asked guardedly.

"Soon a daft old man will be in here to try and save your soul. So I will give the oldest of my gifts, the one I shared often and always much to the enlightenment of the recipient. I will give you the ability to know a lie when you hear it."

William felt a cool hand across his brow. He tried to flinch back but a spasm of pain down his back immobilized him. Tendrils of tingling sensation seemed to penetrate directly into his brain, like cool fingers reaching right into his head and gently rearranging what they found there like an old lady moving around the ornaments upon her mantelpiece.

"Oh hush, that poleax didn't do you much harm," Ahriman said.

Which was a lie. William felt his eyes grow wide. He looked up into the devil's deep black eyes. He felt the lie like a chill down his spine, combined with an absolute certainty of what the sensation boded. It was what it must be like to live your whole life with eyes closed, and then one day to open—the discovery of a new sense.

"You lied," he whispered with amazement, more in that he knew it than that it was so.

"Oh, wise mortal," Ahriman replied acerbically, "I never lie."

With that brief chiding comment, he was gone. Leaving two distinctive slivers of deceit, one for each statement that he made. William rolled slowly onto his side, moaning with the pain that ran down his back and chest. The devil lied. William knew that it was ridiculous he had not given that fact any serious degree of thought. Anything Ahriman said was more likely to be false than true. What did that mean? Had the child been damned, had it been damned already? Was Allen ever doomed to die? Had he in fact lived? Much to William's distress the latter concerned him more. Ever since the death's head had been removed, he had assumed his old friend to be safe, whereas even now they might be laying him out in the chapel with the rest of the fallen. It struck William that there was only one person he was sure would miss him, and who would worry at that absence. If he lived, Allen would worry, and do his best to seek William out. It was a strangely comforting thought.

The door opened at the hand of a tall liveried guard, and admitted a man in black scholar's robes with a bearskin cloak hung heavily over one stooped shoulder. He was a man of advanced age and a shuffling gate, but the sharp eyes that fixed on William were like those of a bird of prey. Time had certainly not fogged the old bird's mind for all that it was doing to the rest of him. William felt hardly prepared to speak to such a man, but apparently he was not to be given a choice on the matter.

"Good morning, we are so pleased to have you as a guest."

The phrase sounded true, except for the word "guest" which rang as a simple lie as well as an irony. William frowned and struggled to sit upright. He pushed himself carefully against the wall, bracing his shoulder against it. His left shoulder would still take a little weight but from the right side and down to the small of his back things were certainly not as they should be. He felt as tender as if his skin had been stripped away and the flesh beneath beaten soundly with an armourer's ball-headed hammer. He supposed it must indeed be the blow from the poleax. It had not hurt much at the time but in the heat of battle such things might not be noted.

"You are one of the Earl of Serle's men?" he asked in a dry whisper.

"Festrigan, his spiritual advisor."

William looked away. "The man who asked that I be captured," he said, remembering the words of the knights on the battlefield.

"I asked for you to be brought here for your own good," Festrigan half-lied.

"But mainly because you want something from me."

"So cynical!"

"But am I wrong?"

William was surprised to hear the old man laugh. "I cannot tell you all of my reasons just yet, but I hope to, in time. When I am sure of you."

William tried to listen to Festrigan, especially as, if the devil's gift could be trusted, the words he was speaking were free of deceit. He was glad of that because the feelings he experienced when hearing a lie were anything but pleasant. William's mouth was dry, his body wracked with pain and his head thumping with a piercing ache that waxed and waned but was only growing with time. The devil has simply laid one further discomfort on him when he needed it least.

He raised one trembling hand to the back of his head and was rather surprised to find it whole, if tender and matted with blood. The bandage was doing little good, being too loose to staunch the blood, which had matted and dried in his hair. It crumbled between his fingertips. William pulled the useless

Emily Veinglory

bandaging away and glared as his visitor as fiercely as his fragile state allowed. The old man seemed to be deep waters, a most unwelcome complexity in William's already chaotic life.

"The earl will give you better care and accommodation if you agree not to attempt escape. All the honor a knight should be shown, in fact," Festrigan said gently. "You might even find it pleasant here. He boasts a fine cellar and woods stocked well with deer. All we would ask is that you speak with me each day on matters that should concern us both, but in which my counsel might be useful to you."

"I do not agree to any such understanding," William said. He was simply too unsure of what was happening to bind himself to any option now, whilst he could hardly think.

Festrigan knelt by his side. "Come now, it is a common enough thing and not thought of as anything but reasonable. Why deny yourself the comforts of the earl's hospitality? I am sure you will be ransomed very soon."

That last was clearly a lie and William shuddered at the feel of it sliding down his spine like a glistening slug. They intended, for whatever purpose, to hold him for some time. That in itself made him firmer in his resolve, but he was beginning to feel horribly dizzy, as if sitting upright was more of an effort than he could currently sustain. Thoughts of who to trust and why, any thoughts at all, seemed to slip away from him before he had properly finished them. He was also beginning to feel distanced from himself, as if he were watching an actor playing his part from a safe dark vantage well back from the stage. William allowed himself to slide gently to the ground, and let his eyes fall closed. He wanted nothing, nothing at all but oblivion. Whatever action he took now would be ill considered and probably unwise, anyway.

"Sir. William?" Festrigan said in a voice made querulous with concern. "William, just give me my pledge so I can bring a healer to see you. Things will make more sense when you are comfortable and rested, and we can speak together properly as civilized men."

William's breaths came in short pants as he felt unnatural warmth spread over his body. Even though his eyes were closed, he experienced the most compelling sensation that he was looking down at his own face. He could see the creases around his eyes, the blood on his cheek where it had pooled under him as he lay, and the flushed luster of his skin as the fever took hold. William was sure that he was well on the way to becoming seriously ill, from whatever cause. Part of him fervently wished to surrender to that illness and leave the cares of the world behind, if only for a while.

He meant to speak to the old man with sarcasm, to say "I am quite comfortable where I am." But when he opened his mouth he was amazed to hear himself speak the truth instead. "I do not know that anyone will pay my ransom."

It was surely not a thing he intended to say, but it was the truth that lay behind the lie he meant to utter. He could not promise not to attempt escape, if that might be his only means for regaining freedom. It was a process of thought that had not been clear to him until he heard himself give it voice. William could only assume that the blow to his head had loosened his tongue or that the fever was affecting his mind. He prayed he would not say more whilst under its influence. In fact the state of his body was slowly beginning to alarm him for that reason if no other. To die was a simple doom, but to be remembered as an evil man would be calamity for his wife, whatever her allegiance. He wished her no great adversity, and the child.

"Nonsense," Festrigan said. "We have sent word that you are with us. The baron has many faults but he would not leave a knight in his service unransomed."

His new sinister sense shivered again and he felt like a ship hitting a cross-wave in the peril of the night. His response suggested that they had in fact sent no such news; for all that Festrigan did believe the baron would honor such a request. They had sought him out for some reason that was not encompassed by the current conflict—they had told nobody that he was with them. But if they meant to keep his capture secret, why did they offer to take his parole and let him wander the keep and even the grounds? Gossip would quickly reveal his whereabouts to anyone interested in knowing them—Allen, if no other. The whole situation made no sense at all, and he was in no fit state to unravel it.

William kept his eyes firmly closed. Matters were becoming too deep for his rattled head to deal with. He wanted to accuse the man of his lie, but was wise enough to keep silent so that Festrigan would feel easy in his speech and reveal other informative untruths. It seemed he might be speaking to this man again and might need every advantage he could grasp. Besides, there was no telling what he would actually say upon opening his mouth, in his current state. Discretion was clearly called for. With dismay, he contemplated that his senses, for all their apparent veracity, might be misleading him anyway—any gift must be judged on its source as well as its contents.

But what Festrigan said next also seemed to be absolutely true, and it came as a great surprise.

"I will come back in the morning, and I hope for your own sake to give you ease and tend to your injuries. I truly mean you no harm, in fact great good. You have been duped by the devil and entered his service. But I will still save you, still show you a way clear."

William curled up tighter but made no reply. Perhaps it was true, perhaps not. That this man knew was a final defeat, his straits could no longer be kept secret and his family name unstained. This man knew. William wondered if it would somehow be possible to trust him.

After all, the devil's gift might be but a lie itself, and meant to further confound him. Besides, if he had given the devil Margaret's child then he was beyond redemption no matter how sincerely it was offered. And how much aid could he expect from this mysterious scholar, more likely he would turn out to be yet another of the devil's pawns or some fool who had no way to fulfill his promises. The balance of his feelings rocked one way and another. He was offered one old man as a source of all his hopes and there was so little left to lose—and yet he hesitated.

William stayed still as he heard Festrigan stand and knock on the inside of the door and question the guard.

"He seems a bit rough. Are you sure he will be all right to leave like that tonight?"

"Oh aye, a knock to the head is a hell of a thing for a day or two. No point even trying to talk to him 'til tomorrow really, he prob'ly won't remember it anyway."

Festrigan came back and William could feel the touch of his regard. Then a musty weight settled over his body. Without opening his eyes, William could only assume that the old man had doffed his cloak and leant it to William as a blanket. It was a small, kind thought and did much to tilt the balance in William's heart.

"Try to sleep," Festrigan said with a feeble pat that was probably intended to be comforting. "The earl has gone to bed for the evening and will not be disturbed, but in the morning I will see to improving your care whether you give your promise or not."

Quite unwillingly, William found himself beginning to feel good will towards the old man for his concern. If the devil's gift was meant make him distrust Festrigan it was hardly fulfilling that function. But perhaps it was meant to do the opposite but without good cause. Such thoughts chased their tails in William's head as he was left alone in his chilly cell, to fall into a fitful sleep.

Chapter Nine

The peace was declared and Allen waited for the lists. In the last skirmish, when it all went against them, he'd taken an arrow in the thigh. It had been prised out with much prodding and liberal application of spirits inside and out, but he was left with an agonizing limp and his man always fussing around with unseemly pillows. It was truly evil the way they made those little barbed arrow-heads to go in so easily and come out so slow and hard, and he could only hope the archer hadn't tainted the head as they so often did. Still, he was left with a leg that could still do the job, and a servant set on saving him any chance to use it. It could certainly be worse, when it came to his own fortunes. Allen was pleased to get away from Yarrow a moment and give some thought to the matter of William's unknown fate.

The defeat on the field came on the fourth day. They'd looked brave enough up to that day, but suddenly it was as if the earl's men fought with the strength of lions. The baron's forces went from holding their own to being pushed off the field in disarray, a complete rout. It had all happened in under an hour, but such balancing points were not so rare in battle. Small matters that might seem of no consequence might give men heart or dispirit them.

It rankled Allen's pride to be on the losing side, for he had done no better than the rest, but the consequences, for the nobles at least, were light. A few paddocks and a bit of useless moor had been taken and taken back—and good riddance to them for they hardly seemed worth a cost, measured in men's blood. Allen would have walked away from the week of combat with few regrets had it not been that he had surrendered to his most foolish impulse to contact William and embroil him in the cursed matter.

Allen had allowed himself to think that he was only doing what Will would want, preventing him from being slighted as a knight and left out of a battle that was rightly his. Fights were important to knights, a chance to win trophies and favors. And Will was not in the king's service, just the baron's. He would have few opportunities to win such favors and had much need of them. That was if he believed Will's version of events. Allen had to wonder what this recent marriage meant. Will had annoyed the baron but pleased the king? That could be a risky prospect as one was much closer at hand than the other, regardless of the difference in power.

Actually he had written for Will because he had simply been lonely, thinking of the days of his youth, the last great friend he had known. Differences in rank excluded him from closeness with the nobles above him or the servants below, and the other knights went where their particular duties called them. Few were together long and even then the knowledge that death might yet part them and the culture of bravado in their ranks limited the closeness that developed. They were fine company for drinking and carousing, but never spoke a word that had any real meaning—they'd die for you without ever knowing a thought in your head or sharing one of their own. Allen might aspire to being a simple enough man to settle for that, yet in truth he longed for more.

The bulk of the camp had vanished away over the last few nights. There was no point lingering after a defeat, nothing to be gained from it. Better to be away rather than be underfoot of a baron angry at the failure of his plans. Even the wounded were borne away by their kin or servants in a haphazard parade of carriage and wagons. The camp followers vanished away to seek their living at the next battle, fair, hanging...or any gathering big enough to bring trade for whores, cooks and thieves. Little was left but trammeled ground, a few forlorn tents, some of them simply deserted as not worth the trouble of carting away. Allen was left with the company of a few dejected souls, the tenant farmers emerging to survey the damage and the carrion crows attracted by the corpses of the horses and a few unrecovered human dead that no one deigned to see. Allen had looked at them all, and closely, but had not found the face he sought, to his relief.

It appeared that the lists had finally been posted. Allen limped over to the boards by the gate to the keep where all notices were posted. The new sheets were those he had been waiting for so nervously and so long. He scrutinized the first, which listed almost a score known dead, young chancers mainly but a few seasoned men. Only the knights were recorded on the list. As many again would have been lost that were simple men at arms or of the other lower ranks. A second sheet recorded those few who had been captured, and there was nowhere on that short list to lose a name. William's disappearance was complete and the sad truth was that one did not lose a captive, whereas a body was far less valuable and far more anonymous. The most likely explanation, by far, was that William was dead and driven down into the mud in some trench or ditch beyond the edge of the proper field. Allen had searched as best he could but it was a lot of land and rough with brush, trees, caves and defiles enough to hide most of an army, let alone one small man.

His spare mount had found her way back near the end of the first day of fighting, exhausted, close to foundering but unscratched and with her tack intact. It had taken her a while as she'd thrown a rein and stuck her foot through it, hobbling head and foreleg together. If only the dumb beast could speak, Allen might have some idea what had befallen Will. At least he now had a hale beast to continue his own role in the battles for as long as they lasted.

Allen stood a long time looking at the list as it fluttered on its nail. The horizon darkened visibly all around him, or at least it seemed to. Stubbornly, his hope did not entirely die, and he had every excuse to tarry where he was a little longer. His younger mare need some time to heal, and he had no desire to return, unwelcome, to his brother's house. He would stay, nursing his leg and his false hopes. He wondered what Hambly would think of that, but he had no reason to begrudge his faithful follower a stretch of barren ground to camp upon.

It was starting to grow cold. There was that tang in the air that presaged a frost. He went very slowly back across the empty, broken ground. Even beyond the very reasonable aches and pains, his leg felt a little "off". Allen had been wounded many times before, often worse than this, but this felt different. Glumly he decided that rest was in order. He could do little more than wait, and may as well do that ensconced in a thick hide before a nice fire. He would do Will little good if the rot took him and he needed to come up with some plan as to what to do. Alive or dead, Will had gone somewhere, and Allen needed to think on how to find him.

"There you are," Yarrow greeted him, as he entered his tent, with ostensible neutrality.

Of course what he meant was, "what are you doing out there when you should be in here acting with appropriate decorum and letting your staff run your errands?"

Allen surrendered his cloak with a sigh and shiver, for the inside of the pavilion was not noticeably warmer than the outside.

"Nothing about Sir William on the lists," he said redundantly, his mood was bound to have given that away.

He sat back on the bed with his legs eased out in front of him. He could hear his other two staff moving around behind the tapestry that divided the internal space. Yarrow's sister was one, not really appropriate in camp but she wouldn't be left behind, and her son Berrick. By the smell of it, the preparation of dinner was underway. Yarrow stoked the fire and laid on split logs with the precision of an expert in the arts of camp. He put more of his infernal cushions at Allen's back so that he could lie back at rest.

"You know the problem of having your dear sister along?" Allen said. "Flowers and birds embroidered upon every surface."

"You should be lying flat," Yarrow replied sternly as a mild reproof.

"I'll settle for the flowery cushions," Allen conceded as gracefully as he could. He was not sure he would win a battle of wills with his surly manservant right at the moment, and he was likely to need his help by-and-by.

Allen leaned back with a sigh and let Yarrow settle a lambskin-lined blanket over his lap. He had little to rightfully complain about so long as life afforded him these modest comforts, indeed most men could not boast so much. Yet there was still an ungrateful part of his soul that insisted it all counted for nothing if there was no one to lie here by his side and rest their head on his shoulder. The meanest peasant must be happy so long as they share their tiny sod hut with a loving spouse and fill it with their children.

Having plans to devise, he meant only to close his eyes a moment whilst the evening meal was prepared...

Yarrow was bending over him with his usual chaste solicitousness. Allen started awake at his familiar touch, discerning that it was full dark, much colder despite the roaring fire, and that they were not alone. A woman stood before him at the foot of his pallet.

She was a small, full-figured and grim-faced girl. Her clothes marked her as highborn although they were worn and soiled from traveling. Not being dead, Allen noticed she was attractive for all that her manner was forbidding. He also noticed the damp mass of her dark and curling hair, and just as he finally realized who she must be, she spoke.

"Sir Allen of Argent, I am Margaret. It is unfortunate that we meet under these circumstances. No, don't rise... Your man told me that you were wounded."

Allen was struck immediately with the impression that for all her beauty and apparent refinement this was a sensible woman, and she would need to be. His first, instinctual attraction to her was quickly transforming into a genuine regard. He settled reluctantly back against his pillows and gestured to his vacant chair. His sleep-fogged mind grappled to suppress his immediate, and most inappropriate, responses to the sudden appearance of such a beautiful women in such a grim place.

"You know that William is missing?" he said, although offers of hospitality should properly have come first.

"I know it," she said. "Although I did not until I came here. The baron has informed me."

She spoke tersely, as if she shared Will's low regard for that man, which was no more than he deserved. The damn baron was not concerning himself at all with Will's disappearance, and he had probably not broken the news gently. Even as that thought occurred to Allen, he went a step further and wondered if Hambly might be the reason Will was gone. He tried to keep that concern from showing in his features, not knowing how easily upset Margaret might yet be at her husband's uncertain straits. Lady Margaret would have enough to deal with without him sharing such outrageous and unfounded suspicions.

An older man came in behind her; it was Shandrick, the overseer of the White Lady Tor estates. Allen had been out there only briefly and many years ago but that man had a most distinctive face, like a disapproving potato. A little less gray and a few more lines only made the effect more pronounced.

"Only Shandrick came with me," she said. "The straw must be cut, the swine are farrowing. It is no time for anyone to be away from the estate."

"It was always a busy little place," Allen agreed mildly, although he knew it could not be her true reason. A few men or a maid as chaperone would hardly be missed at any time of the year.

Yarrow's sister, Finister, came and took Margaret's cloak. She fell easily into the role of lady's maid, which the lady obviously needed, traveling without female companionship.

"William speaks of you," Margaret said. "He regards you highly. I came to be with him, but in his absence, I turn to you."

Allen could only confess to finding that a dangerously welcome responsibility.

"Of course, he replied. "Will is like a brother to me and I hope you will think of me the same."

He prayed that his voice did not betray any other forbidden hopes. In truth, he would never pursue a lady betrothed to his friend but every time he looked at her, the response within his body grew stronger and it as rare that he was so drawn...to a *woman*. Even as she smiled at his reassurance, his heart leapt.

"I can understand now why William puts such faith in you," she said with downcast eyes. "Even though I hardly know you at all, I feel sure that I can trust you."

She looked up at him again and Allen found any possible reply dried to dust upon his tongue. He looked over her shoulder to see Shandrick standing, arms crossed and scowl deeper than it had ever been before. For once he was grateful for that gargoyle-ish man's regard, it reminded him of his proper duties.

"Umm, will you take some wine, my lady? I mean, perhaps you have missed a meal upon the road. I am sure something can be found?" Allen cast a pleading glance to Yarrow, whose own face was set in a quizzical expression that suggested Allen was not acting with full propriety. "Umm, perhaps, you might ask Finister to join us?" he added.

Yarrow stifled a smile and set about making arrangements. Lord knew where he found the chairs and glasses. Margaret refused foods, but accepted watered wine. She bade Shandrick retire to the servants' area, which did not please him.

"Your forbearance, please," she said to him, more carefully than many a lady might. "There is a matter that I must discuss with Allen which is most personal and I would rather have some degree of privacy to do it. I will speak to you of it later but for now I ask that you withdraw, and Allen, I will not trouble your other staff as yet. Shandrick and they shall be close enough to know that nothing improper occurs if they stay beyond that tapestry."

So at the lady's insistence, they were left alone in each other's company with four servants crowded into the other half of the pavilion.

"My lady, are you sure that..."

"Sir Allen, you blush. I am sure the two of us may be trusted for a moment and what I have to say is for your ears alone. I came here to speak to my husband, but finding him gone I am confounded. I need an ally, and I know you to be the one man who has his absolute trust. You will understand once I have spoken that I am giving you mine also."

Allen felt awkward to be stretched upon his couch in the presence of a lady, let alone one who affected him like she did. The gravity of her words finally put his petty reactions out of his mind.

"Of course," he said plainly. "I will hear whatever you feel inclined to tell me, and do all I can for you, as I would for Will."

There was sadness in her eyes when she replied. "'Will'... I wish I called him something so informal, or *dear*, or *beloved*. Our marriage has not gone well. It is not even in the legal sense a completed union, you understand what I mean?"

Allen was slow to understand, and no doubt blushed again. It was hard to understand how any man would neglect to...consummate a relationship with such a women. Even were she not the one you might have chosen, she was unmistakably beautiful and of a sound character and good mind. He simply nodded his reply.

"I did not learn until recently that he was warned against me," she explained. "He was told that I might be sent by the king as a spy, or a means for stealing his lands from his family."

Allen's understanding of the situation began to grow. It would play into William's worst fears—he knew the king had been very angry with his father for stealing away his favored mistress. And the thing he valued the most was the estate on which he had been born. The place his parents had loved and lived in exile upon for over a decade before the fever so cruelly took them.

"Please believe me," she said, almost swallowing him with her eyes. "I do not know what Harild intended, but I have not connived against him. I wanted only to be a true wife to William. Once I heard of the libel against me, I wanted to tell him the truth. I wanted to face, together, whatever scheme may be laid against him. But now there is a no word of him. Where can he be, Allen? What can you tell me?"

"I know not," Allen said. "There are four places we might seek him. On the field, if he has fallen, although I have done my best on that account, with the baron who does not regard him well, with the earl who might have him and not disclosed it, and with the king for little happens without his knowledge."

Margaret's face was striking in every expression it displayed, not least her resolute response to his list of increasingly hopeless options. He might as well suggest they storm the gates of heaven and seek her husband there.

"We may tackle them in that order, I suppose," she said. "If you are willing."

"More than willing," Allen said and he leaned forward to put his hand over hers where it lay on the arm of the chair. He had moved incautiously and winced as the muscle in his wounded leg draw taut.

"But less than able?" she replied.

"We shall manage, between us, I am sure."

In the space of a few minutes, he felt as if he had known this woman for years, and loved her as long. He knew that together, no matter how unlikely it might seem, they had some chance of finding what had happened to William—even if it was the king himself who brought it about.

Chapter Ten

Margaret looked into Allen's eyes. She saw in them a beguiling symmetry, unmistakable honestly, and deep attraction. What a fool she had been to discount love at first sight and what an *utter* fool she was to find it now. She tried to stifle the feeling even as it was born within her breast, but as soon as she had seen him lying wounded upon his pallet her heart had lurched. She drove herself firmly to do as it willed rather than what was wise. She needed the aid of a man, a knight, to find William—she sternly reminded herself—and that was her only goal. She was married to William and that was an oath absolute that could not be undone. She remembered how William had said as he left for battle, that their marriage might be given a second chance. She was committed to giving it that chance rather than lusting after golden-hired errant knights.

Allen frowned. An endearing crease appeared between his eyebrows like a comma on the open page of his face.

"I am sorry that I can tell you so little," he said.

"We shall learn more, together," she said. "I have this feeling that the two of us together will be a formidable force."

If only she could channel her regard into proper sisterly amity, Margaret believed that might be true. Between those who would not insult a lady and those who would not turn away a knight, many doors would be open to them. Allen leaned back with a sigh, seeming to bring their conversation to a close.

"But what about tonight?" he said. "You will stay in the baron's household, surely?"

He looked to the main flap that served as a door where nothing but a chink of darkness showed. Suddenly they were both mindful that it was becoming late and they must go to their rest.

"No," she replied from immediate instinct, but then she explained, "We simply cannot trust him. I may not be safe there. He might, for example, insist upon acting as my protector and I would end up locked safely away until I was declared a marriageable widow." She saw him wince at that last word and pressed on. "Together we may yet find him. My name might get us an audience with the king, if needs be. But the two of us must not be hobbled by the concerns of petty gossips. We shall deport ourselves honorably and those who will talk, will talk. It shall not stop me, if you can bear it also."

She was pleased to see him taking her perspective seriously. "Well, we must have a chaperone and some arrangement that is seemly, but my concern is only for you. Very little is expected of a single man and I do not worry over much about what is left of my good name."

His frown deepened, and truly it was hard to see how the situation might be worked without causing Allen any distress on her behalf. A degree of respectability must be maintained if they were to be received by those they would need to see, in seeking William. There was a difference between being bold and cutting their own throats before they had even began.

"You lady servant shall serve as chaperone," she suggested. "And if needs be, I shall sleep in the carriage, it is secure enough."

"No," protested Allen. "I could not possibly allow a lady to do so when I stay here in comfort."

"While I will not suffer to have a wounded man cast out of his own accommodation. So we shall both stay here, the men in one part and myself with your female servant in the other. That must be proper surely?"

"That is quite improper," Allen said with a sigh. "But if you will suffer it, I dare say William will understand we acted in his interests and had to be pragmatic in our arrangements."

Margaret was surprised to find Allen so willing to abide by her decision, and hoped that William would indeed understand. For unlike Allen, he knew full well that she was capable of infidelity—and in truth Allen would be enough to lead any sensitive woman astray. The wine made her feel drowsy and dislocated as she stood. This somewhat scandalous arrangement was the best solution they could come to and it would have to do. If Allen was willing to take her lead, she might yet have her opportunity to open her heart to her husband and be his wife in truth.

"Tomorrow I would see the field of battle," Margaret said, trying to feel as bold as her words. "And we shall make our plans for the days to follow, but now I feel I need my rest. We have been a long time upon the road and my bones still ache from it."

Margaret was deadly tired and her mind was becoming dull. Her whole spine was jarred from the road and her neck felt too tired even to hold her head aloft.

"No, my lady," Allen said with apparent alarm. "Please take my bed and I shall send Finister to see to you."

Margaret winced to see how stiffly he stood and hobbled as he left, with apparent pain—but a certain amount of gallantry must be allowed to any man. She allowed him to take himself away and could not quite suppress her feeling of loss as he left her sight even so temporarily. She sat gingerly upon the bed, still warm with his body's heat. There was a subtle smell also, clean but musty like any space where only men were normally found. Margaret's mind drifted into a place quite out of keeping with her mission. Her experience of men was limited and hardly inspirational, yet her imagination more than made up for that lack. She clenched her fists and forcefully turned her mind aside for fantasies conjured up by the thought of lying in a bed not quite so vacant of its owner.

A servant woman slipped into the room uncertainly in the wake of Shandrick hefting the trunk that contained Margaret's hastily chosen clothes. She could not recall whether she had thought to include a nightdress, but if not a chemise would surely do.

"I shall settle the horses," Shandrick muttered.

Whether that needed doing or not Margaret did not know, but she was quite sure Shandrick would wait 'til everyone was settled for the night before returning through that main flap to assure himself that she slept in a chaste bed before returning to his own. Margaret did not resent the precaution. Shandrick was William's trusted man and if he felt she had behaved well enough then William might well believe it also when—God willing—they met success in finding him alive, and the time came for the question to be raised.

Margaret was pleased with the understanding she had reached with Allen, and sure their confidential speech had been necessary for achieving that accord. But she wondered exactly what he had might have failed to tell her. She, after all, had said nothing of the illegitimate child she had lost, nor of the rumors that the king was her father. Either fact might make her role as spy to plausible just when it was imperative that she win his trust. But her conscience itched at having not disclosed so

93

much. Now it was too late, for her lie of omission was established almost beyond retraction.

She sighed and thanked Finister sincerely, who brought her water for washing and ordered her things. She went to her rest, forcing her mind to settle on William as her last thought of the day. William, wherever he was, *God protect him.*

But it was not his dusky looks that colored her dreams.

William sat upon a sparsely padded chair before an empty grate. There was another chair beside his where old Festrigan sat. As was so often the case between them, silence reigned. With time, William had come to trust his ability to tell lies from the truth and read the many shades between, but to his distress that extra sense came with a caveat. He could not speak a lie, and whenever he attempted it, he found his lips expressing the corresponding truth instead. Thus he had said very little indeed. He recalled tales of men who consorted with fairies ending up this way, and now he understood what a curse it truly was to have to conducted yourself only with full veracity.

The topics Festrigan had raised in trying to draw William out could be divided roughly into three groups. Firstly there were the things that Festrigan said and believed to be true. The old man thought he was a servant of God and wanted to rescue William from the service of the devil. That was an admirable goal, yet it begged the question of where the old man got his information, and just what he thought he might be able to do. If that had been the end of the matter, William might well have been tempted to confess all and throw himself upon the scholar's mercy.

But then there were the things Festrigan said but did not know to be true. He assured William of the earl's goodwill, although William had yet to even see the man. Those assurances were as hollow as tongue-less bells. The more William thought about Serle, the more he wanted to know what that man thought and how he fitted into his advisor's schemes. Some nobles were very predictable men, ruled by simple virtues and predictable because of it. William had heard that the Earl of Serle was such a man. If only William could get to him.

Finally there were things Festrigan said boldly but knew full well to be untrue. He said he was motivated only from a desire to help William. But beneath those protestations an ulterior motive obviously lurked. It was something else that motivated the old man, that burned within him. William wanted to know that thing, that great looming unspoken thing that shared the room with them like silent ghost.

"Will you not speak, damn you?" Festrigan finally snapped. "If I knew you wished salvation, I could risk telling you how to achieve it."

His word slanted towards mistruth, as if, perhaps, the old man was not entirely sure how such a salvation might be achieved. William, for his part, thought it unlikely such a thing were possible, if he was truly responsible for the death of a child. He would not confess the depth of his sins; he would not grasp for false hopes not matter how sympathetically they were presented. And yet what did it gain him to sit here like some forgotten invalid as the empty days wended past? William groped for a proper plan...but to form one he needed to know more.

"Why don't you tell me what you really want?" William said quietly.

"The devil has twisted your mind and made you suspicious of the one man you should trust." Festrigan leaned forward; his shaggy brown brows arched into a sharp V of earnest entreaty, but his intensity merely made William more wary.

"You have not told me the whole truth," William said plainly. "And I cannot trust you until you do."

He tried to hold the ideas he wanted to convey very clearly in his mind, and to be absolutely sure of his belief in their veracity, to avoid them twisting between his teeth.

"Are you such a man of absolute truths?" Festrigan challenged.

"I have lied," William admitted easily. "The last thing I said to my comrade before the charge was a lie, I lied to my wife when I made my vows. The prince of liars has an apt disciple in me. But we are not speaking of me. We are speaking of you, and when you say you brought me here to save me, you do not speak the whole truth. Thus, I cannot trust you for I cannot know what you will do, and what will flow from those actions. I may not be a virtuous man but there are those I care for, and I will not blunder into harming them, or aid those who might bring them harm."

Festrigan leaned back again and hunched deep into his fur cloak. Having finally goaded William into speech, he took his time considering the words. William waited patiently, turning his eyes to the empty fireplace. The balance of his heart leaned to trusting the old man, but more rational instincts forbade such foolish notions.

He had to admit that Festrigan had been good to his word in having William's wounds tended, and bringing him to a room a man might take a few paces to cross. He had a sleeping pallet now, which was soft, and there was even a window he might open to the sky. It provided a vantage that was easily five tall stories from the ground, down a sheer and inward facing wall, and so this consideration offered no escape from anything but life.

William still felt frail and he was not steady on his feet even five days after receiving his injuries, and he could not focus upon his discourse with Festrigan for long. The old man had been solicitous and spoken with him less than an hour each day as he edged towards his purpose. And that was the crux if it. William felt the old man had a purpose. But was it a higher Godly purpose, the service of the earl or some delusion of his own? Festrigan was up to something and so a pact with him was not something to be entered into blindly.

"I shall try and tell you what I can," Festrigan said in a tired and quavering voice that plucked at William's sympathies. "But how much can I share with a man in the service of my enemy? I think the devil has a purpose for you, a specific purpose. He grooms you to make a choice and he may present to you in many guises. But if you choose wrongly, you will bring disaster to every man and woman alive and many yet unborn. That is what I think, and I cannot afford you to let you continue to blunder down the primrose path laid beneath your feet."

William looked at the old man, his diction enlivened now by a fanatic's fire. There were sparks in his eyes and for all that his words were vague, his belief in them was strong. But in his fervor he looked like an even more doubtful savior, for old man can fix on strange beliefs in their final years and cling to them beyond reason. He might well believe what he was saying, and still be wrong. William pursed his lips as he looked at this, the only option offered to him, with some distaste.

"I find it hard to believe that I am so important," William said.

Festrigan threw up his hands in exasperation. "As you have said, why do I go to such trouble to talk to you? I can tell you what to look for, and when the moment comes, what to do. But I must know that you seek the path of virtue or all I will do is instruct you in how to carry out the devil's work all the better."

"You want to know if I wish harm to people, damnation to our world. Of course I don't. Tell me how to thwart the devil, and I shall do it."

Now it was Festrigan's turn to pause. He watched William long and hard until, abashed, William looked away again towards the wall.

"Alas, I do not believe you," Festrigan said.

William merely shook his head. "Then do not bother to share your fairy tales with me," he said. "But how long do you mean to keep me? I want to speak with the earl. I want to know why he has not ransomed me. I wish to leave this place."

He had come very close, but in the end he did not see anything in Festrigan that he could trust, or use. William had not seen the devil since first waking at Serle's keep, and perhaps he would never see him again—he could hope so. What he wanted most of all was to walk away from here and do all he could to compensate Margaret, be she true or not, for his behavior towards her. Let her spy, let the baron seize his lands, but let him prize them from the dead hands of a true knight who defended what his father gave him unto death. William would no longer play his betters' games, be they barons, kings or the devil himself. Once he won his way clear of this prison, he would go home to White Lady Tor and there he would stay.

Festrigan stood and wrapped his cloak about him. The chill in the room was someone's idea of punishment for William withholding his payroll, and William fancied that he knew who.

"Who told you that you were not ransomed, your master?" Festrigan snapped.

William's truthful tongue was beginning to escape his control again and he heard himself reply, "You told me so, when you lied about it."

Festrigan took one backwards step but did not protest. Instead he said, "The earl will not speak to you, he leaves that task to me."

And that also was a lie, although not one absolute. "Ask him, for until I see him, I will speak no more to you. I think there is some madness in you, and not all that you speak of is real."

Festrigan's head jerked up stiffly. "This from a man who converses with the devil."

William did not reply. He turned his eyes stonily back to the fireplace. There was one uncertain virtue that William knew he had in full measure—stubbornness. In his thoughts, there floated many replies. "As you believe I do?" "As you pray to God" He did not utter them. He would say no more until he saw the Earl of Serle and knew his status as a captured knight. He would ask for no more than his freedom and he would offer anything he could to secure it.

Chapter Eleven

"I spent a long time looking all down this side," Allen said as they surveyed the straggling tree line along the edge of the ragged field. "It's the only aspect with a good degree of cover. The only place I couldn't really get to is down that ravine but I could see most of it from here and it's a narrow stretch."

Margaret looked across at his bleak expression and wished she could match the depth of that emotion, but she did not wish to feign it. She could easily imagine him scouring these verges and defiles in a dogged search for his foster brother. He was almost a perfect compliment to William, being built quite small and pale with a naturally open mien. Life would be different if she had been betrothed to such a man. But that was an unproductive thought. Marriage was an irreversible condition and better she repair her marriage than try to wish it away. She had, after all, made that oath and it was hers to live with and make the best of.

There were cattle grazing on the field now, starting to prune back the range grasses of the neglected commons. They watched with blank expressions as Margaret and Allen rode past, and did not stir to flee. Margaret wondered idly where they'd been during the fighting, hiding in the trees or stabled away in some barn chewing their way through straw they'd need when winter came. The battle had come and gone here with no more lasting effect than a passing market or a fair, but for the men missing, or dead. Cattle grazed on grasses flecked with blood as if nothing of note had happened here.

"It's a larger area than I would have thought," she said, looking back at the field. It stretched away over a gentle slope and over the horizon.

"It's got to be big enough for a lot of men, scores, to move about. For charges and melees, attacks and counterattacks. You see, when one side is driven off the field, back to their camp, or killed so that they'll never return, that's when they count as defeated. So it has to be a good distance to go, an emphatic distance. It's best everyone agrees on the winner."

Margaret turned back to the overgrown defile. "You didn't look all the way down there?"

"It's the only place the horse wouldn't go and I couldn't, and I don't think..."

Margaret kicked out of the stirrup and unhooked her knee. It was a pleasure to be out of the sidesaddle, which was putting a kink in her back. Between the hard carriage seat and that ridiculous contraption, it would be a wonder if she ever stood up straight again. Sometimes she wished she could sit astride like a man and face the way she was going rather than craning all the time over her shoulder.

"Margaret, what..."

"I'll start as I mean to go on," she muttered. "Thoroughly."

The steep slope of the crevice was like a wrinkle in the hill, thickly thatched with nettles and saplings. She waded though them and started to slide down the treacherous drop off into the dark recess of the land. She hadn't been anywhere more wild than a knot garden since she was a little girl, but it couldn't be too hard to climb down a bit of a hill. Having begun, she was certainly not going to turn back and let Allen see her act the feeble woman when they were off to such a good start.

"Margaret, be careful."

She had been riding a solid gelding, trained to draw and ride—he'd had duty pulling the carriage on her journey. He was obedient to a dropped reign and stayed where she left him. Allen limped behind her but stopped where the ground became steep. She wrapped her hands around the roots of the tree and skated further down the slope. Her wet fingers slipped and she dug her fingers into the wet clay to get the rest of the way down. It took quite a while to get to the bottom with Allen fretting at the top. Shandrick and Yarrow caught up with them after covering the other edge of the field one last time. Margaret had spent the morning with Allen looking over the ground, and she had to agree that even though the area was considerable, there were few places that might offer concealment.

"This wasn't my idea," she heard Allen say with comic haste.

Surprisingly, Shandrick made no protest. "She's a strong enough girl it seems," he said. "She'll be fine. The better for having something to do after what's happened."

She supposed he did not know how clearly the words would travel to her ears. She prayed that Allen would not hear the layers of meaning in them. Shandrick, after all, was bound to know about the child. Staff inevitably talked to each other and there was almost nothing that happened at the Tor he was not privy to eventually.

Finally she reached the bottom. It was a mire that was not properly a stream, with amber-tinged water seeping through a morass of silt and rotting leaves. She sank up to her shins and was pleased to be wearing her boots today. She looked up and down the bottom of the small cut and saw very little but undisturbed weeds and a fallen log.

There was something about the shape of that log that seemed awry, and so she waded through the sucking mud towards it. Clouds of small flies flurried about her face and as she drew near, the impression grew stronger, and gradually she began to see that the sodden mass was not the carcass of a fallen tree but something altogether less wholesome. In the brown flap at the top there was stitching showing, at the bottom of a boot. A small expanse of grotesquely swollen flesh, an upturned face disfigured at the eyes and mouth by some kind of gnawing creature. It was a pitiful sight, a man dead and left so long undiscovered,

"Margaret," Allen called. "Are you all right?"

The dead man's hair was brown, a mousy color, as was the beard that strangled down from the remnants of his chin.

"There's..." Her voice came out impossibly small so she ventured to begin again. "There's a dead man down here. It's not William."

"You're sure, my lady?" Shandrick replied nervously.

"Quite sure."

Margaret looked all around again, for any place that might conceal a man. Then she turned and began to climb up the other side where she might gain a different perspective. She felt quite calm. Shandrick and Allen were nearby, and a dead man could do her no harm. She looked up towards the light and sighed. At a distance, warfare seemed a glamorous business in which the righteous triumphed and the virtuous never came to any harm. Now, as she stood in the gloom and smelled the miasma of rotting flesh, it seemed such a pointless endeavor.

Still. This man, who had fought and would never fight again, was not William. Margaret could picture his long-featured face as he leaned over his correspondence or pored over some crampedly written text. She smiled. It was reassuring to know that even the stifled excuse for wedlock that they had shared was enough for her to feel joy that it had not been him left in wild stream for beasts to feast upon. Somehow she was sure he was alive, and if she could just find him, everything would work out for the best. She still could not say that she loved him, but perhaps if he allowed it, she yet might.

As she neared the top, Yarrow and Shandrick offered their hands to help her up. Margaret would have preferred to find her own way, but did not want to spurn the gesture. She put her muddy hands in each of theirs and was pulled up into the daylight. She could see Allen standing just beyond, backlit by the noon sun.

"Yarrow and I should go down and get that man out," Shandrick said. "There will be people waiting on news of his fate also."

They shambled off down the way she had come, and following her path, they could hardly miss the poor man. She did not envy them their task. She was acutely conscious of being left alone with Allen in relative privacy. He was likely to take too much advantage, holding the reins of his own skittish mare and having picked up her gelding's also. He looked rather bashful—but when he spoke, she knew his mind had been on something else entirely.

"It could have been him," Allen said gloomily, "and I'd have not looked. How could I have put my comforts before..."

"I think our best course is to steer clear of might-have-beens," Margaret said firmly, with more than a few of her own. "What *is*, gives us quite enough to deal with without mithering about the might've's."

Allen considered her with a look that might have fit on one of the wandering cows. She needed to shake him loose from his pointless recriminations.

"Come on, Allen," she chided. "What do we do next?"

Allen's expression became determined and alert as he turned his thoughts to more constructive ends. "Logic would suggest that Baron Hambly might have caused something to be done. But I would focus on the earl next."

"Because..."

"If Hambly is responsible, he will have acted in stealth and will be difficult to detect, and if he has done anything, forgive me for saying so, it is murder—and that cannot be undone. If Serle is our man, it might be a fairly innocent mistake. If William was captured, but they were careless, or he caused some offense or was too ill to say who he is, he may be held by them and no one aware of it. It makes most sense to go to Serle next as if William is there, he will be easily found and he may be found alive."

Margaret was pleased to hear him speak plainly rather than resorting to pointless euphemism and avoidance on account of her sex. She resolved to be as frank in return.

"So why did you not go to him before now?"

Allen seemed to take no offense at her question. "I am a man alone, an enemy in the conflict and not in the role of any legitimate representative of Hambly's forces or William's kin. I would not be admitted to Serle's hall, nor would my queries be entertained. But you are his wife and due all reasonable aid and comfort, and I am your protector. We may now go most boldly to the earl's door. If he turns us away, it is against all protocol and as good as an admission of guilt that all may see. Whether William is there or not, it is a place to look where we will be admitted."

"Shall we go today?"

"To make the matter as plain as can be we should arrive early in the day, a reasonable hour to be received. I know it is frustrating to allow delay, but it would be better to go to him tomorrow and bide the night here if you can bear my company so long."

Yarrow and Shandrick could be heard rustling around amidst the underground, cursing at the state of the body and the smell as they moved it. Margaret put one hand to her mouth as she imagined what they must be doing.

"I can bear your company, I think," she confessed. "And if it is the wisest course, it is what we should do."

Allen's seemed to light up at her reply. Just as the two men appeared, each pulling a stiffened leg of the corpse as the bloated body scraped along behind them. Margaret looked away, seeing no benefit in catching sight of his ravaged form again in better light.

"Leave him there," Allen said as they heaved the body out onto the meadow. "Hambly's men can find him there if we let them know. It's his job to see to the men that have died on his account. We can go back past the keep and meet you back at the pavilion. It will give me a chance to let the baron know we will be leaving in the morning. I dare say he will be pleased to see the back of the both of us."

"Oh aye," Shandrick said.

Margaret was rather surprised at his willingness to leave her alone with Allen. But she knew that he and William both rated this young knight most highly. And he, at least, had the old man's trust. She made no comment as she let Allen help her mount. And if it seemed that his hand lingered a moment too longer on her calf than was necessary to steady her, that was probably just her imagination. She let Allen lead the way as they headed back to the dismal hump of the hill on which the keep perched.

Margaret was in no hurry to speak to the baron again. She had found Hambly abrupt in his treatment of her the previous day, and she would watch him closely as Allen spoke to him now. As a women, she was supposed to have intuition, and she would be doing her best to apply it as she looked at the baron's repugnant face.

Their horses picked their way along the boggy path to the keep. Allen dismounted in the sand court at its center and tethered both their mounts to a ring upon the wall. He looked to Margaret and she nodded for him to proceed. They were allowed though to the main hall without challenge. It was a much quieter place now and the baron was still there, taking his luncheon whilst speaking with his counselors.

"Ah, Allen, one of my valorous knights," Hambly called out drunkenly, his voice dripping in sarcasm.

"If my presence displeases you, I have good news. I will be removing it from your lands in the morning."

Margaret tensed to hear Allen speak with such hostility. It was never a good idea to make a nobleman your open enemy. Hambly just waved his hand in dismissal, but Allen had not spoken his piece.

"We found a dead man at the far corner of the field," he said. "One of our own pike men by the look of it. And only yesterday you assured me none of our forces were, in your own words, 'lost or misplaced'."

Hambly lurched to his feet, his mood changing quickly. "I do not answer to you, you poor excuse for a knight!" he roared.

Margaret was surprised to see how foursquare Allen stood against him, and how calmly. She had assumed he would speak as Hambly's servant, not with such an open air of accusation.

107

Emily Veinglory

She reached out and put one hand on his forearm. "Sir Allen," she cautioned.

"Listen to your whore," Hambly slurred as he turned away.

Allen strode forward and slapped Hambly hard across the face. The room fell deathly quiet, and the situation escalated out of control. Such quarrels lead to duels and deaths even more pointless than those accrued in battle. Fights over empty words and petty honor.

"You insult my brother's wife," Allen said in a tone that seemed almost casual in contrast to his actions.

"Do not cross me. You are my man; I do not answer to you."

"I am the king's man, leant to your endeavor which has now ended. Withdraw your insult or be called to account for it."

The silence stretched out as the counselors looked on, their faces crinkled with amazement, amusement or concern depending on their perspective. None offered any advice to their master. Margaret felt sure that were Hambly sober he would not have spoken so. His bleary eyes wavered between her face and Allen's, his brow creased with befuddled rage.

"I could have you killed," Hambly slurred.

"Aye, and would it be the first time you had resorted to such methods?"

"I meant only that my champion could best you easily if you insist upon the duel on this creature's behalf." Hambly sounded a little pressed and uncertain now, as if that was not at all what he had meant, but belatedly he was seeing how things might look once word got out.

"Well," Allen said as he backed away, "you have not accepted my challenge, so I shall have to assume you'll not defend your uncouth and drunken slur. I'll not tarry and press

108

the matter. I have a brother still missing, and I will search for him until he is found."

Allen spun on his heel and reached out to Margaret. She put her hand demurely in his and they left the room together. Margaret was sure to walk as tall and hold her head as proud as he did. She began to understand how deep this man's bond with her husband truly was.

"Was that wise?" she whispered as they ducked out the low stone door.

"Not wise, but it may stir him to action, or at least start rumors at his expense. It also means I have said clearly for all to hear how things stand between us. If Hambly has done something without honor, any who know and disapprove might now seek us out to tell their tale."

"Had you planned to do it?"

"Not planned, no, but it seemed right and I did it. Time is running out and caution will not always serve us."

Margaret squeezed his hand. She could not agree more. Then she pulled her hand away from his and stepped apart.

"Some caution perhaps," she said. "I would not like to be burying my husband's brother and left without any man of my class to turn to."

"I am rebuked," he said with a smile. "I shall be more careful in future."

"Be serious."

"I am most serious, the baron's champion might not concern me, but your disapproval would surely cut me to the quick."

He looked to her with exaggerated sorrow and mournful eyes, and Margaret could not help but laugh.

"Come along," she said. "We'll get everything packed away for traveling tomorrow.

Chapter Twelve

Ahriman contemplated Margaret as she sat beneath the scant domesticity of a knight's campaign tent. She was wearing a demure gown of pale gray velvet and watching Allen polish his tack, but only with the most covert of glances. She generally occupied her eyes and fingers with a piece of tapestry that she carried with her, by long instinct. No women of the court would every be seen without a piece of "busy work" close at hand to give her a pretense whilst gossiping, or an excuse to ignore less than pleasing company. Not so this time, rather the reverse. It was a fitting piece, depicting the White Lady of the Tor, a notoriously faithful wife from local myth. No doubt Margaret was pleased now to have something to do other than worry about her missing husband and her all too present protector.

It had been an impulse on Ahriman's part to place the Bridle in her hands, but he made it a strict policy to act upon impulse whenever one arose. With time, one action in particular was becoming more appealing. Yes, he had long decided that the Regent's Bridle must be kept in hands that would not use it, or in no one's hands at all if need be. He did not particularly want dragons usurping his place; no matter what delicious chaos they might sow as they went. Yet there a certain interest created, a certain piquancy to his own idle games, by putting the Bridle in the hands of one whose reactions would be almost impossible to judge. That would be William; as he became more desperate, he would become more erratic also. Ahriman was sure that if he placed the Bridle with Margaret or Allen it would inevitably come into William's hands as despite the finer (or lower) feelings they might have for one another, both of them sought William as the heads of flowers seek the sun.

In Serle's keep, Festrigan was baiting William again. Ahriman could know that without being there, even in his currently depleted form. The old man had the crystal with him. The scholar hoped that if God blessed his intentions, the sphere would show William something to sway his mind and win his obedience. Festrigan wanted a follower, as much as he might think he had higher motives, he tired of pursuing his fixed quest alone. Yet William was proving a most unobliging acolyte, as well he should, given that he already had another, more impressive, master. Ahriman smiled a private smile as he strolled invisibly about the small pavilion. On the whole this small play was proving tolerably amusing.

As Ahriman watched, Margaret tightened a stitch and bit off her colored thread, and a fitting diversion occurred to him. Forming a picture in a sphere is a simple thing. Far simpler to make one of a whole cloth than transmit one from far away. William was becoming uninspiringly inert, and there was one sight that might stir him into action. It was a sight not so far from truth as to be difficult to imagine. Two hearts and two bodies imagined it right here, although the various tethers of duty and obedience prevented it from being realized. Yes, Ahriman decided, time to sow a little discord with a most amusing mistruth. If it were not spoken aloud, William would not know it for the lie it was.

Ahriman drifted upwards, as gentle as smoke, into the cloud-shrouded night. He let the breeze take him down the tree-lined road to Serle's estate. The earl's palace was not a castle, it was meant to be deserted if attacked in preference for the less opulent and more chilly residence farther towards the center of his lands. But this residence was a far more pleasant building than Serle's gloomy and neglected fortress. It was extensive and still soundly made of solid granite, but low to the ground and stretching out in three wings across beautiful gardens. It was punctuated by four ancient towers that the later building bridged together. Three stood at the terminus of each wing and one, the largest, stood at the center. Near the apex of that broad tower, like an embowered damsel, was William. During the day he had a reasonable view of Serle's gardens and reserved hunting land that stretched as far as the eye could see, even from that height.

Festrigan held the crystal sphere on his bare hands as he sat at his accustomed seat. His mild manner was slipping even further as he become impatient, fretting that the Bridle might be slipping from his grip—when in fact it was coming ever closer. That was the irony of men's blinkered lives, so often their own efforts confounded them the most.

"I have spoken to Serle," Festrigan said. "He will see you tomorrow if that is your insistence. But you may find it unfortunate to press that case. He is not a patient man, and he thinks you know something that he wants to know. I am prepared to convince you to confide in us. Serle's methods are inclined to be considerably more direct."

William, true to his intent, said nothing. After initially being drawn to the dour old counselor, William now began to harbor a suspicion that he was simply insane. There were many cunning and plausible kinds of madness, he knew. Festrigan watched him too avidly and was too vague in his beseeching to be quite rational, and William wanted no more to do with him. He wanted Serle, a noble and a knight. This would be a man he might understand, who might speak plainly and even be bargained, or reasoned, with. Although, if in the end he also wanted this secret that William did not possess, it would be for nothing.

"So this may be my final chance to convince you by gentler means," Festrigan said testily. "And so I shall act as boldly as I dare. I make an admission to you in this. I have long owned this stone I have here, and long used it. It shows men that which they seek, whether they know they seek it or not. I want to know whether you will take it in your hands, with me here present, and look into it. If you will do this, I will bother you no more, and not return here to your room unless you call for me."

Ahriman stood unseen between them as Festrigan passed the sphere to William, who accepted it with some reluctance. He was tired of Festrigan's rambling, but he had no other company and did not greatly enjoy the long hours alone with his conscience and the aches of his tardily healing body. William held the sphere between his hands gingerly, and looked at Festrigan who leaned forward eagerly. He hoped that William sought the Regent's Bridle, and that the sphere would show where it lay. William thought that all he sought was escape from this tower, and thus was more than happy to be shown the means of accomplishing such a feat. Yet he considered more likely he would see nothing, that only a deluded man would think he saw visions within a stone.

In truth, Ahriman knew that poor William, orphaned young and raised up lonely, was seeking something else entirely—and Ahriman decided to show it to him, after a fashion. William took a deep breath, gave Festrigan a disdainful look, and then gazed down at the translucent stone. For a long moment, he saw nothing but a distorted view of his own fingers. Festrigan having used this device only in isolation had no way of knowing that it showed its visions to one person, and not to any other audience. Nor could he know that its true purpose was to allow

114

witches to send messages to each other by their own will and imagination. It did also detect chance emanations for things or persons touched by magic rather than being its source, but that was not its intended purpose. Ahriman caused a picture to form, but for William's eyes only, Festrigan saw only a gray and swirling fog no matter how he beetled his eyes to pierce the cloudy darkness.

...Margaret's skin seemed dusky against the strangely delicate pallor of Allen's chest. She lay in his arms, wreathed in disarrayed hair and simple woolen blankets. They lay peacefully entwined together in the languorous repose of the sated. Margaret's head pillowed on his shoulder as if that were its natural home. Allen stirred and looked down on Margaret's sleeping face. He smiled gently and drew the blankets up over her naked shoulder. His hand came to rest, lax and gentle, across her shoulder and his eyes drifted peacefully closed again. Allen seemed so openly happy, Margaret so entirely at peace...

William's fingers cramped tight as he stared at the uncanny vision before him. It faded slowly from sight as if obscured by layers of sheer fabric falling before him. Festrigan leaped awkwardly to his feet, sparked by desperate strength.

"What do you see, where is it?"

He grabbed for the stone savagely, trying to see into its heart. In his haste his fingers were clumsy and stone slipped from his grip and fell upon the hard hearth. With a curiously muted sound, it shattered. It was as if the strange device was tired, and surrendered its existence quite easily and quite completely, with nothing more than a shivering sigh. Festrigan was left looking down at a pile of tiny shards, none much larger than a grain of sand. They stirred under a faint draft and cascaded down into the bare floorboards.

Festrigan shook his head as he staggered back. "For the love of God, what did you see? You must tell me, you must. So much depends upon it."

William put one trembling hand to his mouth and remained mute. What little he could truthfully say, he would never utter, nor would it ever give Festrigan the answer he so desperately wanted. Whatever the old man sought to see, he was sure that was not it. He was not without sympathy for the old man's plea, so sincere and so important to him, but if he wanted his answers, he would simply have to learn to look elsewhere for them, where they might be found. William turned away again, almost expecting that Festrigan might strike him. But such violence was simply not part of his nature, no matter how provoked he felt.

"Well then, go to your audience with Serle and his inquisitors," Festrigan hissed. "He may have you, and with my blessings."

The old counselor stormed across the room, banging loudly on the door for the guard to release him. Ahriman was most pleased. William should look closely at Festrigan; if he had carried on his current path, he would become a similar sort of man. Ahriman's involvement in his life might bring it to a precipitous end, but at least he would be spared that fate.

William sat quite motionless and contemplated what he had seen with a sort of stunned calm. He waited to feel anger, but it had not followed. No, he did not actually want to feel anger, it was just a sort of obligation in this kind of circumstance—one's best friend and wife seen in bed together. But in the last few days of contemplation, he had gradually realized what a fool he had been in his treatment of his wife. Whether she had been sent by the king or not, she was a young woman, tied to him by deep vows and left alone with him upon an isolated estate. He should have been open to her. He might have won her over. He might even have won her loyalty and, if he deserved it, her love. What it must be like, to hold someone like that... What love must be like.

She had strayed once, but it was clear now that the child of that indiscretion was no more. He pondered the possibilities. A child's life was uncertain, a woman's will had a way of being done. Most of all—if the devil wanted the child perhaps he saw no need to wait for it. That was the most likely thing. William had caused the end of child's life, unsaved and unshriven— casting the poor might into a most absolute and immediate damnation. Given the depth of his own damnitude, his wife's indiscretions seemed so petty. That was why he felt no outrage against her, no anger at Allen's complicity. Compared to his own actions, they were not so unreasonable. They hurt only one person, and even then, only if the truth were discovered.

And Allen, well, he was as he was. William was only slightly surprised that he did not draw a line at his foster brother's wife. Indeed, unconsummated, the marriage might still be annulled— and that might be for the best. William looked down at the white dust of the stone, as it continued to lazily drift into the gaps between the boards. The shards seemed even now to be breaking into smaller and smaller pieces and he should not be surprised if it soon disappeared altogether. William had, until recently, not had any firm belief in magic. He had thought such things properly part of fairy tales, like dragons or angels. You see them written of, of course, even in books that present themselves as history or autobiography, but if you never see them around you in the world, they just cannot feel real.

Perhaps he had treated love with that same disdain. He heard tales of it, even of his own parents although his most fickle memory preserved them only vaguely. But it did not seem plausible that any women would deign to feel such a strength of emotion for him, let alone one commanded to his side by a man who opened hated William's father.

It was, perhaps perversely, comforting to contemplate that if he died Margaret might take guidance from Allen, might even marry him like the old pagan custom where a younger brother was meant to take on his elder brother's widow. People capable of love should be allowed to find it wherever they could.

William supposed that it was degenerate and evil for him to think of such things so calmly, yet there was no rage in him and it felt more virtuous than sinful, more compassionate than wrong. Gradually he turned his thoughts to his own circumstances. Whatever Festrigan thought he knew or had, or could tell them, William was in possession of no such secret. The man had obviously turned to witchcraft, and that unwholesome art might well have perverted his mind and caused him to believe many strange things. What was more important was whether he had convinced his master. If Serle thought the same and would use ungentle methods of interrogation, well, William could tell him nothing. It seemed very pointless to stay and suffer such indignity.

William went to the window and swung the shutters inward. The scene beyond was almost entirely black, with just a few spots of reddish light shifting between the swaying branches of intervening trees to show where other window lurked, and other, warmer, rooms. William could see a world where his own foolish choices would do no further harm, where Margaret would be free to seek a husband who would treat her better, and the devil would have to find a new puppet to play with. Again, he observed in himself no excess of emotion; he

118

was like a cracked vessel where any fear pouring into him simply leaked out again.

But he knew that his courage might be transitory or frail and that if he did not act upon the moment, it might be lost. He put one foot upon the broad sill, paused only a heartbeat, and stepped out into the void. He closed his eyes and prayed that he would not linger, that Serle would present his body merely as a misplaced carcass of the battle slain.

The sensation of falling was...wrong—still and warm—and William was back inside his prison room with unpleasantly familiar arms about him.

"Not so soon," Ahriman said. "Or would you accuse me of being so unsubtle a bane. You will not die until I permit it. And I will not permit it until you no longer amuse me."

The devil's face had an aspect like alabaster, his expression a frozen displeasure that should have struck William with deep terror. As he spoke, it seemed like there was another voice behind the voice William heard, one less than human with the sibilant hiss of a giant snake and accompanied by the clashing of great and jagged teeth. But once a man has surpassed his fear of death, he is not longer easily afeared. If there was worse to face on the other side, then William was ready to discover it— for the consequences there could be his and his alone, not shared with those who disserved it less or not at all.

"Will you tell that to the earl?" he said in a bold voice despite his shaking body. "He may yet deprive you of your sport."

"You have your wits," Ahriman replied, more in his usual jesting tone. "You have your allies, and you have my gifts. Foresight of death I have given you, awareness of lies, and this also. I give you freedom from pain. You shall never suffer from it again, and so need not fear. But beware—I shall soon ask you for further payment for my indulgences, but here is one more. The stone did show you what you were looking for. If you can fathom that, if you ever fathom that, I will release you. Do you understand?"

With that he was gone, leaving William to discover new depth of despair. He had not understood, at all.

Chapter Thirteen

Serle tended to believe Festrigan's wild tales about this mysterious object, the Regent's Bridle. Festrigan just had a habit of being right about things, no matter how peculiar his ways and Serle was not inclined to bet against him now. What he could not fathom was just what made the damn thing so important... And then there was the undeniable fact that for all his intelligence Festrigan could not be relied upon to keep things in perspective. So what if the person who held the Bridle could tell who was a true descendent of Lukas, the first king of Ordran? That was an ability of most dubious worth from any perspective Serle could imagine. And that was the problem, wasn't it? Serle would admit to having many sterling qualities as a nobleman—loyalty, perseverance, intelligence even, but never imagination. He was almost proud of his stolid and traditional ways.

Serle paced the length of his receiving chamber as he contemplated the issue, turning it this and that way in his mind. He was not by preference an overly active man except in the pursuit of game of one sort of another, so he knew that this pacing reflected how worried he truly was about they way he had handled the issue of Festrigan's knight. He had just sent for that young knight, Sir William of White Lady Tor, but he was not entirely sure what he should do with the man. Sir William had apparently not been amenable to Festrigan's methods of persuasion, which stayed delicately short of force despite what Serle commanded. And if it fell to Serle to take that kind of action, he wished to be sure of his ground.

Festrigan said this man sought the Bridle, might know where it was, might have been told where to find it, might even have it hidden somewhere. Serle shook his head. That was a lot of "mights" and he had never cared too much about the damn thing, until discovering last year that the king, his patron, was not of legitimate birth. He had been slow to admit the truth of it but the gossip that swirled around the courts was damning, even the most loyal had come to believe it in their private thoughts if not their words.

The child, Harild, had been born almost fifty years ago on a country estate near the coast. Queen Isabella had gone there ostensibly because her of delicate health; her health was indeed poor and the excuse held for a very long time. The child's birth had been kept secret for over a month, and they had not returned until he was a robust toddler not discernibly too large for his reported age. But the servants who had been bribed still told their stories here and there and slowly, very belatedly, the truth was leaking out. The servants at that estate had been few and loyal, but those who were but children then, potboys and sweepers, grew into an age where service did not quite mean what it once had. Or perhaps it was just that the adult servants were of known and true characters but the children as yet unformed. Some had finally grown into a greedy or destitute middle age and they had begun to talk.

The queen had clearly conceived the child whilst the king was abroad, visiting his cousin who ruled the small but rich island nation of Laporte. The child was most definitely not his, although not even the most keen-eared gossipmonger could give a firm account of his true paternity. That was not a matter too many dwelt upon for if the child was not the king's, the exact identity of the interloper mattered little except to the king—by now long dead. Opinions differed as to whether he had known there was a cuckoo in his nest. In accordance with a long and unhappy tradition of the crown, he cared little for his wife.

If he had learned all this back in the beginning, it would have been enough to make Serle change camps, which might have been enough (in those delicate times) to put a different man on the throne. There had been a plethora of cousins, upstarts and open bastards jostling for contention, many of whom had a firm claim to descent from Lukas—and some sound support amongst the nobles. Serle had never given them a moment's thought; in those times he would have backed the legitimate heir even if he had the charm and skills of a deformed piglet. Experience had softened that fixity....

But he was longer in the tooth now and more pragmatic. Serle was a man well pleased with his current situation and not inclined to act rashly. Harild was somewhat older and also a king any man might be satisfied with, but for his lack of an heir, and that could hardly be said to result from a lack of effort on his part. Just a sickly wife he was not overly fond of, and a great many daughters. Lines bred true too long weakened, Serle knew that from his horses and hounds. These delicate princesses and their weakling ways offended Serle's sense of husbandry for men or beasts, perhaps it was best to have some bold rake's blood in the higher lines, to give them vigor. If only he would have a son within wedlock and settle the matter. Serle did not want to see his hard work undone before he died. There were, no doubt, some bastard sons about awaiting their chance to make horrendous trouble, should the current situation endure until his majesty's demise.

Serle fretted as he waited, pouring a measure of sweet liquor despite the early hour. It would be simpler if he could just concern himself with matters of his own estates and doing as the king bid, regardless of his reasons. He had sent a missive to Harild when William had first been taken—but it must have arrived by now and the lack of reply must indicate the king's disinterest. Serle was left to make his own decision for good or ill.

Still, the significance of this in terms of the Bridle was clear, a holder of the Bridle would know that Harild did not carry the blood of Lukas and was not a proper heir to the crown. Serle had suffered through several uncharacteristically sleepless nights, but in the end he had decided himself. Harild had proved himself a good king. He was cunning in the extreme, committed to his nation's wellbeing and compassionate to his people. He had ruled over an era of unusual peace, prosperity and justice. In the end, Serle was a kind-hearted and pragmatic man. Whether the kind of man who accomplished this benevolent rule was son of a king, or son of a goatherd, was not in the end important. Once it was done, it showed he was a man capable of ruling, and if God had disapproved, the land would have suffered for it. Serle took the fine harvest and the good fortune of the land to indicate that God condoned the rule of Harild, and Serle was not a man to disagree with God.

So this William might use the Bridle to claim Harild was not a legitimate king, but who would listen? Since he had first discussed the matter of this William, Serle had experienced something of a change of heart. After all, any man who used this device and admitted it branded himself as a witch and therefore an evil man much inclined to lie and act to damage the realm. No, Serle was not going to make any great effort to secure the Bridle; he saw very little point in doing so. But he did not want to alienate his old and useful advisor Festrigan; especially as many of his able followers regarded the old man with an almost superstitious awe. Serle was still reluctantly inclined to put this William to torture, if only to placate

Festrigan, but it was a decision that did not sit easily with him. He had no compunction against using such means, but preferred to have a better reason—one he truly believed in.

Two armored guards admitted William and the lengthy wait was apparent in seeing his pallor and uncertain gait. He stood not only restrained at each side by the guards, but also surreptitiously steadied and supported by them.

"Wait outside," Serle commanded as he scrutinized the man at the center of his little dilemma.

They hesitated to do this but complied. There were, after all, other guards outside the window and only door, and little in the room that a wounded and unequipped man could use as a weapon. Serle hoped they would also take into account that he was a strong man and quite capable of looking after himself for all that his stoat body and considerable size did not give him the appearance of a soldier. His rank required men-at-arms always around, but he firmly believed his abilities made them a matter of decoration not necessity.

Serle indicated a seat that faced his writing desk, and took for himself the wooden chair on its other side. He regarded William for some time and was somewhat intrigued by what he saw. He was a tall man, slender and quite young; his conformation gave a gangling impression overall, though Serle knew men with this appearance might be stronger than expected. William's complexion was dark and his expression suggested a man with a strong will and abilities beyond his years. Serle was much inclined to take this young knight seriously, rather than fall into the trap of underestimating him simply because of his youth and provincial roots.

"So, Sir William," Serle began, "are you a truthful man?"

William's naturally mournful expression was broken by a wry smile. "There is one thing you may depend on from me, and that is that I will speak the truth if I will speak at all."

Serle was beginning to believe him, no matter how unlikely it may be. William had a way of speaking that was devoid of bluster or considered pretence. Serle had no patience for fencing with words or weaving pretty nets of interrogation. It was his strategy to be blunt and direct, and it tended to serve him well.

"So do you know what it is that my advisor Festrigan is seeking?"

William looked across at Serle with an open expression that immediately made him seem much younger and more vulnerable.

"I know he seeks something, although he does not say what and I do not know. Whatever it is that he wants as far as I know I cannot give it to him. I am quite ordinary for my station, humble even. I cannot think of anything in my power or purvue that warranted your actions or his. So I cannot give this mysterious thing to you either, no matter how you ask me, or how often."

Again, Serle was disposed to believe him. What he saw before him was a simple knight, and man not given to intrigue. Festrigan sometime chided Serle for trusting far too much in bonds of chivalry. But for all of that, his intuition was quite good in matter relating to other knights, even if it did not extended reliably to other sort of men, nor certainly women who were an absolute mystery to him with this vaporous ways.

Serle continued almost glibly. "Have you ever met the devil, William? I am told you might've."

"A man would be a fool to admit having any truck with the devil. But we are not always given a choice of who we meet— only what we do once we have met them."

This suggested a deeper man; Serle's attention was drawn fully back into the discussion. He could only assume that the evasion meant that William thought he had met the devil. In fact only a fool might do other than lie under these circumstances. A fool or a very honest man indeed.

"Wouldn't he just?" Serle mused. He was not sure how to continue and decided to desert that topic for now. "If you could topple the king, would you do it?" he asked sharply.

William thought in silence for some time as Serle watched him sharply. Finally he replied.

"I have no love for the king as a man, he persecuted my parents for petty and personal reasons. I am sure you are aware that my father married the woman he kept as a mistress. But I would not argue that he is a poor ruler, and I would see no benefit to deposing him and leaving the land laboring under a disastrous interregnum."

"I think you may actually be an honest man," Serle said sourly. "I am surprised."

"I may yet be able to say the same."

Serle was inclined to take affront at the implications of that, but he was patient and made no quick reply. Young William was not going out of his way to be obsequious, so he must think he had something on his side. And there was little he said that Serle took offense to as yet.

"Tell me what I should do, then?" Serle said with an indulgent smile. "I may have a man before me who knows something that might damage the realm. I may have a man before me who is in the service of the devil. What kind of man would I be to release such a creature? How could that be justified?"

"You are an earl," William said with calm acceptance. "You serve the king. I am a knight and serve my baron as he serves the king. I think the only duty I owe the devil is to thwart him, and the duty you owe God is to perform as an earl should. What do we know of magic? What does it all have to do with us? Perhaps, it is a mistake to be drawn into such matters and I want nothing more to do with this thing you seek or any matter best left to my betters. My most humble advice to you, which may mean little under the circumstances, is this—do only as you know you should."

Serle felt disturbed at the ease with which he believed this man's veracity and the sense that his words made. This young William might not be the direct as he seemed, just extremely deft in his manipulation and aware of how to best exploit Serle's doubt. But this did not necessarily make his argument less true. What did Serle know about magic and devils? It was not properly his business. He was a competent earl, and a loyal follower of the king. And only the king should command him, not the wayward concerns of his advisor, no matter how well-intentioned.

A servant entered with the cowed expression of one most reluctant to intrude. He came right to Serle's side and bent to speak lowly into his ear.

"Lady Margaret asks to be admitted. Lady Margaret of White Lady Tor."

That decided him. It might well be a terrible mistake that he was about to make. But it was wrong to seize a man from the field of battle and hold him in secret. It would be a blatantly wrong thing to deny the fact to his wife and turn her away, after she had come so far.

"Show her through," he said, knowing this gave him only a minute or so.

After the servant had left, he added, "I shall release you now and we shall agree not to speak ill of each other in any way, even as you say, if this means saying nothing at all about the matter of your time spent here. I shall disappoint you and make a lie to cover it. I shall say you were knocked senseless a long time and only now recovered. So it is most fortuitous that your wife has come to reclaim you. She is a gift to you, I believe, from the king—and as his most loyal follower I would not wish her to go away empty-handed. Do I have your bond and your agreement on this?"

William's watched him quizzically for a long moment. "You do," he said at last.

And just in time. The door burst open and a woman entered in advance of any servant to admit her. This was no wan princess but a robust maiden with a mane of twisting tresses. Her gaze swept over Serle and fixed on William and she surged to his side and knelt beside his chair.

"William," she said. "Thanks be to God."

He smiled gently in return and put his hand with chaste restraint over her hand. They both looked to Serle, no doubt eager for more proper reconciliation once they had their privacy.

Serle stood. "I am happy to commend Sir William to your care," he said. And indeed he felt easier in his decision for how far astray could a man go with the love of a good, strong woman like this? Serle briefly considered that that good fortune had long escaped him, and perhaps it was time he took steps to ensure he would not die a widower, with only his brief and chilly marriage to his name. "He has just now recovered enough to let me know who to return him to," Serle said warmly. "And here you have saved me the trouble even of sending a message.

Will you accept my hospitality? It is yours as long as you wish it."

Serle's door guards stumbled in the lady's wake, and through them came a man who was presumably her escort, a knight with the blue chevron on his tunic. Serle searched his memory to recall who carried that device but the name eluded him.

"My thanks," William replied. "But I would prefer to return home, with your permission, my lord."

"Of course."

Serle anticipated a most difficult encounter with Festrigan, and was pleased and unsurprised that William would leave him with all haste.

Chapter Fourteen

As he walked into the earl's receiving room, Allen was stunned in two completely conflicting ways. First in that there was William, sitting at his ease in on a tapestry chair, only the back of his tousle-haired head was visible at first but Allen would have known him from any angle or vantage. Second there was the state of him, which became clearer as Allen drew closer. In six short days William had been transformed from a stern but hale young man to a wane and shadow-eyed figure— an obvious invalid. It was easy to believe that he had been knocked into some senseless or confused state and unable even to name himself. But Allen felt an element of skepticism, for every knight was known to some others of his number, be they friend or foe, and marked by his house sigil wherever it might be painted or sewn upon his possessions.

Allen was not, however, inclined to argue. He went to William's other side and reached his arm around his shoulders. He made no more than a nod to the earl as he helped his old friend to rise. William's hand went to his brow as if it pained him, and Allen could see a swollen and black-scabbed wound towards the back of his head. Allen wanted nothing more than to get his friend away from this place, to somewhere secure where he could rest and feel safe. It was as if he thought the great good luck that saved his beloved William might yet snatch him away if he were not vigilant and swift.

"'Tis as well we bought the carriage," he said quietly to Margaret. "Best we away whilst the light is good and make some distance upon the road."

She stood at William's other side and William put his arm easily about his wife's shoulders as if there were no strain between them. He looked from her and to Allen and for a moment he seemed more himself, despite his frailty. He looked Allen in the eyes, easily, and smiled. Allen felt a sensation pierce his heart that was quite familiar, although he always managed to forget just how exquisitely it pained him to love where love was not fully returned.

"Let us go then," William said warmly but weakly. "If you will wait a little for a proper explanation?"

Margaret and Allen agreed readily and took their leave as briefly as they might. Between them they took William down the long halls and out the cascading stairwell into the cinder covered court for the main entrance. Boy servants held the bridles of carriage horses, guards at the doors watched with stifled curiosity as they slowly navigated the stairs and went across to the carriage with the fresh cinders crunching underfoot. Yarrow sat at the driver's seat, and Shandrick, ever cautious, waited upon his mount with Finister's boy, Berrick, beside him, looking small on a full-sized gelding. Each of Allen's followers looked a little unsettled and alert, as if unsure of their welcome and their ease with which they might depart.

Shandrick was obviously startled to see William and his state. Allen waved him back from coming to their aid. "Let us get a little way from here, as quickly as we might," he said.

Finister opened the carriage door and they clambered inside the cramped interior. William and Allen took the forward facing seat and the ladies sat opposite. Allen saw how much Finister already changed with her new duties as Margaret's attendant, reaching out to clasp Margaret's hand as she entered. Yarrow released the brake with a jerk and they left the court at a seemly walk, but quickened to a trot upon the drive. Allen winced at the jarring motion of the carriage and he kept his arm tight about William. The clatter of the wheels at this pace made speech nearly impossible.

Allen leaned forward slightly and shouted to Finister. "Tell Yarrow to take to the commons and find some level ground out of the main way. We will not travel far today."

She nodded and leaned out the window to shout out these instructions to Yarrow. William leaned against Allen's shoulder, drained of strength. Margaret took her own cloak and draped it over William's shoulders and Allen pulled it so that it sat securely. She looked to Allen with a troubled expression; perhaps she also sensed that something was wrong with the entire situation. But as William had said, explanations could wait, now that the worst of their fears had proved groundless.

After a spell of jolting travel upon the common road, the carriage shuddered as the horses suddenly slowed and as the noise of their passage dulled, other hooves could be heard. Margaret craned to looked behind then out the window. Her hand strayed forward to rest on William's knee and he raised his head slowly as if it were very heavy but showed no particular curiosity as to what was happening.

"It is a messenger," Margaret said with a frown, "in Serle's livery."

"We should go on," Finister ventured nervously, "with haste." She was bolder now and quick to pick up on Margaret's mood, for she also obviously itched to flee this new complication.

Allen shook his head. "Yarrow is right, rein in. We couldn't out pace a mounted man even if it were wise to attempt it. It is just one man, we will hear him. It may be nothing, indeed with just one servant bearing the news, it can hardly be a matter of great import."

The carriage slowed and the messenger came abreast of them. He pulled a small scroll from his tunic and offered it through the window without a word. Allen was relieved, if need be most written messages could be ignored.

"I do not wish to detain you, my lord, this word came for Sir William just now. And so I was sent after you to ensure it reached you."

"My thanks for your trouble." Allen said in obvious dismissal. He took the message and turned to William. "It has the king's seal." The man obviously had no instruction to wait for reply or otherwise tarry, he turned back and cantered down the road.

"Open it then," William said wearily.

"It is addressed in your name."

"Open it, or have Margaret do so. Whatever he has to say affects your lives as well as mine."

Allen did not feel he could break the seal in William's name, but passed the scroll to Margaret, who took it nervously and with a puzzled glance to her husband. Truly it was becoming increasingly difficult to see how two people essentially good and sensible had not found any accord with each other, even if it fell short of love. She broke the wax off in one piece and unfurled the small scroll. Given the spare scrap of vellum used, it could hardly be an expansive letter. Her gaze flickered over the words, devouring their content in one bite.

"The king summons you to court, William. He says no more than that."

William sighed and leaned his head back on Allen's shoulder, a place where it felt very much at home.

"What shall we do?" Margaret asked, twisting the scroll between her hands. Given William's response, it was Allen she addressed the question to.

"We must go," Allen replied. "Of course we must, there is no alternative."

"Well, perhaps," William interjected softly. "Allen, if he does not name you then you might find a better way to spend your time then traipsing after us."

Allen shook his head. "If you will have me, I will go with you."

"Of course," William replied as if that was never really a matter of doubt, just an offer that needed to be made. "I am sure we are both aware of our good fortune in having your support and assistance. I just worry that you might trespass into the king's bad favor on our behalf."

Allen turned to see that William's eyes were drifting closed again. Allen had seen many an injured man in such a state, it was as if the body needed all its strength to heal and every action brought immense fatigue. William should be going home to convalesce at his leisure upon his own beautiful estate, but it seemed that was not going to be possible.

Margaret's gaze flicked from William to Allen. "Of course," she echoed. "Very much so."

Allen smiled at her and drew William's body against his own that he might sleep if he were able. "But not today, I think," he said. "We will take some rest, and take to the road tomorrow, early. I do not think that the king can complain at that?"

"No," Margaret agreed. "It would not be wise, I think, but we cannot risk angering the king of the matter is urgent, either..."

William said nothing. He did not seem asleep, but just not inclined to rouse himself to speak. He should not be hastening to the king's side in such a state, yet it was not a summons one could ignore or prevaricate upon.

Yarrow steered them carefully off the main road and down a narrow and winding track to a bumpy byway that terminated eventually in a small dell from which no egress was broad enough to admit them. He could be heard opening a casket stored on the roof and brought down cushions and blankets whilst Finister opened the door on their pastoral resting place. Allen looked out and saw that the clouds were breaking with midmorning and the day was warming quickly. There was deep grass all around and sheltering trees. It seemed like Yarrow had chanced upon a perfect place to break their journey. The way they had come in could barely be seen now that the grasses and small bushes had sprung back into place over the overgrown pathway.

"If Sir William would rest here on the bank. We shall make a camp here and bring him wine and some broth to strengthen him."

"Good man," Allen said. "William, come along, we can rest here today."

"I wonder if we should really go on," Margaret said weakly.

"Tomorrow," Allen assured her. "Tomorrow will be soon enough. He cannot know exactly when the message reached us or how well the road favored our travel."

They took William to lie upon the blanket and Margaret laid his head upon a cushion and wrapped a warm blanket about him. He stayed quiet and seemed relieved that they did not press him immediately for news of what had befallen him. But as Margaret fretted at making him perfectly comfortable, he caught her hand.

"Truly I am not entirely feeble," he said. "Nor so deserving of your care."

"I am the one who decides what I will do," she replied. "I hope you will believe that, for I have always been my own woman, not at another's command."

"Not even mine?"

"You are my husband and so I should obey you, and I will do my best although it is not my habit. But perhaps a wife's highest calling is to look after her husband's interests rather than follow his commands?"

William sighed but it was with humor. "I am more fortunate than I deserve," he said and he closed his eyes again. "I need just a little rest, to regain my strength. Perhaps we can travel a little further in the afternoon."

"Perhaps," Margaret said in a tone that suggested that she thought otherwise.

Margaret stayed by his side whilst Allen helped to settle the horses, but Shandrick and Yarrow shooed him away after a while. Hobbled by his injuries, he was not that much help, anyway—and they were both the kind of serving man who took any assistance in their tasks as criticism rather than courtesy. So it was hardly surprising they were getting on well together. Shandrick as the older took the lead, and Yarrow seemed not to mind. Allen went back to William's side, uncertain whether he would be interrupting him and his wife. But he found Margaret standing and looking down the small valley with a wistful look in her eyes. She turned at his approach and they looked down together at William's still form.

"I think he is asleep," she said. "I do not want to disturb him."

Allen looked down at William face, which seemed quite peaceful and lax. "A blow to the head is a tricky thing," he said. "Sometimes just a bruise, sometimes..."

He watched carefully for breath and saw William's chest rising and falling in a regular if shallow rhythm.

"Sometimes a death?"

"I did not mean..."

"I know. He received this hurt some days ago and he has lived. But it certainly still pains him, especially, I think, with movement. I wish my mother was here, she knew her herbs and healing ways, but I was a poor student. There are so many things I might have learned if I had paid more heed as a child."

"'Tis in the nature of children not to," Allen said with a smile, for the same was certainly true of him. He had been always off on some misadventure, leaving William alone with the tutor—although the both of them were inclined to lie on Allen's behalf rather than wear his father's rage on the matter.

Finister brought a warmed goblet of wine. "Well," she said softly, "sleep is the best medicine." She passed it to Allen instead. He held it, smelling the sweet vapors that rose from its surface. Finister left them alone again, perhaps too quickly—he wondered what she thought she might be interrupting.

"He does not seem angry that I have come," Margaret said quietly.

"He seems most pleased," Allen agreed. "Should I leave you..."

"No, please, sit down and speak with me. Surely, he will not mind that we are here together. Who else in the world is more concerned for his welfare?"

Allen sat gingerly upon the bare ground, with William's prone form between them. The others went about their routine tasks, collecting wood, cutting grass for the horses and fetching water.

"What can the king want?" Allen mused. "He has been most indifferent to William for all his life, and now he sends a summons. Something is going on, and I cannot discern what it is."

Margaret frowned and sat upon the ground beside William, drawing a corner of his blanket over her knees. "I wonder," she said. "I wish I knew. I feel like there is a great dance going on all around me but I don't know the steps. Perhaps it is best this way, we can be direct and blame naivety. I will ask the king why he gave me to William and why he summons him now. I'll ask directly, as I should have when I first received the news of his intentions. I want to know who here is doing the king's wishes and what those wishes are. I hope to God he does not wish us harm, because I do not know what we might do in that case. His power is deeply entrenched and very broad..."

"Why would he bear you or William ill will?"

"You know how he was about William's mother, Katinka. When she died, he wore black to mourn her for almost a year, it was a terrible scandal. I don't know if he would see William as his father's son or as his mother's. I do not know. I wish I did. When he told me he had arranged my marriage, I thought only that he wanted to be rid of me, to send me as far away as he could within the realm."

"Why would he want to do that?" Allen asked, wondering if this was in fact the heart of the problem.

"After Katinka there were other mistresses. One favorite was my mother, Erica. And there have been rumors that I am the king's daughter. I cannot know if this is true, as my mother will not answer that question and forbids me from even putting it to the king. But even so there are rumors. And that is enough to mean that Harild may be safer if I am away from court, and married."

"But he has summoned you back."

"He has summoned William. The message has only just arrived, at least a three-day's journey. He cannot know that I was here to receive it when I should by all rights be back at the Tor like a good and demure wife. He meant to summon only my husband."

"Well then it is fortunate that we are all together. We will support each other through whatever follows."

Margaret looked at him most seriously. "William gave you a chance to evade this trouble, for it is most likely to be trouble rather than anything that can be turned to advantage. He knew you would not take it though."

"As well he should if he knows me at all."

They sat together companionably, looking down to the small level area where Yarrow set a fire and Finister prepared a modest luncheon. Berrick edged over to peer at William, a man he must have heard much of but never before seen. Shandrick scowled and came to pull him away, but paused to look down a moment also.

Margaret was turning some small ornament in her hands, and wearing an expression of contemplation. Allen wanted to ask what the small golden object was and why she had brought it with her, but he did not interrupt her thoughts. He tried to convince himself that the affection he felt for this kind, bold-minded women was nothing more than feelings for the sister he never had, feelings for a brother's wife. In truth he rather suspected he was falling most ironically in love. Was it possible to truly love two people at once? And even if it was, what could be more ridiculous than loving to people that he could not court, not least because they were married to each other.

It seemed to Allen that they were quickly bonding together around William, as if somehow foreseeing that he would need them. Allen shuddered to feel the hand of fate upon them all, and prayed only that there be good fortune with the bad.

Chapter Fifteen

William was washed up from a fog of sleep like sodden driftwood on a grating beach. He hardly knew what to expect when he opened his eyes but he knew somehow, even before he remembered where he was, that Allen was nearby. All through his life until these recent terrible days, if Allen had been there he felt able to be brave, he felt to some extent secure for he never doubted Allen's love for him. If anything he felt regret that Allen loved unwisely in that William's heart held to tight to its responding passion, no longer permitted expression. Poor Allen received so little in reply for all that he gave so freely of himself.

William stayed still, as if still asleep and opened his eyes slowly. He found that it was dark. He could hear a fire crackling and see its uncertain light reflecting Margaret's face as she worked her tapestry needle in deft swoops. She seemed so peaceful at her task, like a Madonna but that her child....

"It is late, you should have woken me," William protested drowsily. He ran has hand across his face to wipe his bleary eyes. He felt his shoulder muscles pull achingly taut, still healing from their outrage, but beginning, at last, to properly answer his commands.

Allen blithely answered from some place behind William's back. "Perhaps this is one of those occasions where we chose to look after your best interests rather than follow your suggestion."

William eased onto his back and pushed down the over-warm blanket. His head was clearer now, not swamped with chiseled pain with every tiny movement. He felt like protesting the delay, but thought better of it. He needed to speak to both of them plainly whilst the initiative still rested with him. Ever since the devil had thwarted his act of desperation the previous night, he had felt sure that he was doomed, his only hope was to leave his great friend and his dependents in an orderly and settled state, both materially and personally. He just hoped he had some little time to achieve that.

"At least you have each other's company whilst I am so ill-disposed. And I am sorry to have worried you and that I will not be able to tell you exactly what occurred. I made a solemn oath to the earl that I not would discuss anything that happened between my capture and when you found me. It was a condition of my release."

"William," Allen began sternly, but then he faltered. "Was that entirely necessary?" he ended awkwardly. He obviously wanted to speak more sharply but was too chivalrous to do so to a weakened man or before a lady. "Is that an oath you owe to them to honor, or one made under duress?"

"I thought it a reasonable bargain at the time, and I am bound by it now," William said as apologetically as he could without showing any sign of conceding.

Allen tried to argue the matter, as mildly as he could as he knelt beside a prone William. "Could you not tell us in confidence; it may have relevance to the welcome we might expect in court. If not myself then Margaret who is as one person with you now before God."

"I made this agreement with my eyes open and I will abide by it," William said. "I am sorry if you find that frustrating. I did only as I thought necessary." He heard a pompous note in his voice and tried to soften it. "Truly I am sorry. I just don't see around it now. I should have had more faith that you were coming from me and that I could afford to bide my time..."

He stopped short of saying he wished he could explain the matter fully; he was not entirely sure it was true and therefore not sure what he would end up saying. It was, after all, a convenient silence that kept the door shut on many other matters. All things considered, he would rather leave his friends in the dark. He would not expect even Allen to forgive his dealings with the devil, let alone Margaret. He was not ready as yet to raise many topics, not least that of the child.

Margaret's nimble fingers were still, now, but she said nothing. Allen shrugged and struggled to adopt a sanguine mien.

"I will not argue with you," he said as if he wished he could. "I have learned the futility of that over the years. But I am not pleased to be blinkered. You cannot tell me Serle's behavior has nothing to do with this sudden missive from the king. But, well, had I been in your place I am sure I would have done the same. And I hope I would act as you, keeping my word as my bond— for all that I might wish now that you were not quite so honorable."

"I think it more likely to be Hambly who has involved the king," William suggested. "But I did what I thought best and I will stand by it. I thank you for you understanding."

Allen's expression softened. "If you think you must keep to this pledge and that Serle deserves such consideration, I will not nag at you about it. You needed to do as you must in the enemy's keep, and alone. I am just pleased to have you back and I think you could behave quite outrageously and not overstep my current indulgence."

"I am cruel enough to depend upon it from you both," William said. He reached out each hand, one to Margaret and one to Allen. "My old friend is used to my presumption, my wife is an altogether more noble creature for I have never been a friend to her..."

Margaret replied in an even but open tone as she looked him directly in the eye. She seemed a rather different woman from the diffident bride he had left behind, a girl he would never think would take it into her head to chase after him or call on Allen, a stranger to her, for protection. "You had reason to think the same of me, I suspect," Margaret said. "But you would be wrong. I am, and will always be, loyal to you."

The subtle sincerity of Margaret's words settled over William like a comforting hand, but he wanted to be entirely sure. "You do not serve the king before me?"

"I do not. We are joined by marriage, William, and I hope we will serve each other most of all."

William nodded solemnly and turned to his right where Allen knelt. "And our most faithful friend, dear Allen, I do hope you will find me a reformed man. I have neglected you, behaved strangely and I can only hope to do better by both of you. Nothing pleases me more than to see you friends to each other. But, Margaret, I hold to nothing. You came to me as a stranger and I have given you no reason to love me..."

Allen made to leave, but William tightened his grip.

"William, you two should speak in private," Allen protested. "I have no business being privy to such matters."

"No," William said firmly. "We are in this together and I hold you no less dear than a man might regard his wife. I make a pledge to you, both of you, and I would have you hear it together. It is a difficult thing I pledge to do. When I speak to you, it will always be the truth, even if that should seem hard or cruel, and I want the same from both of you. And I want you both to hear what I want to say."

"Of course," Allen replied rather too easily.

Margaret looked to Allen. "I have no objection either," she said.

William addressed himself to Margaret. "I ask that we be friends," he said. "For now I think it would be foolish to think of more."

"William, I am sure that we will..."

William scowled at the impending lie, no matter how well-intentioned; Margaret was even less sure what their future held—even less sure than he.

"You cannot be sure," he said more sharply then he should. "I am used to be being alone and have hardly shown you my best aspects. I want to be at pains to make myself most clear. I have no expectation of you. We have done as we were bid in marrying, and more than that is a free choice each of us must consent to, and I do not hasten the choice. However, things might resolve themselves I do not pressure you. You might need to have a little patience with me too. I truly am a solitary creature and must have time to become used to my new situation."

"William," Margaret chided. "You been excruciatingly clear. Do you think yourself so poor a match?"

"Perhaps I do. Perhaps I have reason to. Some few folk find something to love in me and do not think they are richly rewarded for their trouble. Best we be as you say, excruciatingly clear to each other, and to our dear friend. We two are but recently met for all our circumstances. So tell me, can we, do you think, be friends?"

"Yes, I truly think we can."

She spoke the truth. William sighed his relief, tension leeching from his body, and he released their hands. He almost wished he might take their hands and put them together, giving them to each other openly. He had tried as best he might to lay a way for two who loved each other to do so freely, or so it seemed, as far as circumstances allowed. But to suggest this, would be more than they would willingly hear. He did not want to face their rank denials. He only hoped Allen had not acted lightly, but out of true regard. They seemed warm to each other, and William did not think Allen would bed his friend's wife, even if it were not a proper marriage, except out of a deep regard—except for love.

"Good," he said. "That is good to know. A man is fortunate to have two such friends. Now tell me you will be honest with me as much as you can, not matter even if it might hurt me."

"William, what are you saying?" Allen said and William feared he might suspect his true eventual purpose. "We have said as much already."

"I say what I say," William replied. "Can you abide by it?"

"You're a strange man, Will," he said, "But if you want to hear me say it again I will. I'll tell you the truth if e'er I know it, and not hesitate."

"I also," Margaret added. "And perhaps you'll humor me now, and have some of this broth Finister is bringing us. It may not be a proper toast for ardent pledges but it will serve you better."

Finister approached them with a tureen in her hands. "'Tis not as warm as it might be," she said. "But I thought to wait until you woke."

"Most courteous," William said. "I shall do my best to be appreciative of your trouble but my constitution is not as it should be." In fact the smell of the meaty broth was not appealing.

"'Tis only of the mildest ingredients." she assured, laying the tureen down and taking a bowl from Yarrow who followed her. "I hope you will find it doesn't disagree if you take no more than you want of it."

Allen had a knack of drawing skilled and loyal staff to him; for all that he could afford only meager wages. William wondered exactly what awaited them in court, but he had no complaints as to the people who accompanied him there. Allen helped him sit and Margaret moved the pillows to support him. Their care was almost painful to him for he deserved it so little having taken from the one a child, and from the other a woman he might otherwise have married. He saw them smile to one another and felt a deep regret that the world was not a simpler place, where they might simply have gone with one another and left him to his fate, for between the king and the devil it was bound to be a terrible one. If there was only a way to accomplish that, he would do so and without hesitation.

He strove now not for himself, but for a world that he could see after his passing. He could see Margaret at White Lady Tor, with Allen by her side in proper wedlock and these loyal servants around them. It was a goal worth fighting for as hard as he might, worth fighting the devil himself. His own fate did not bear dwelling in, the devil himself was overseeing his doom.

❧

Margaret had put her needlework aside; she could see Finister bringing more bedding so they might sleep that night upon the ground. The sky was clear and a deep color of indigo with night falling. Shandrick had proclaimed that it would stay fine enough to sleep without cover and all had agreed that would be pleasant to do so long as it stayed warm. In truth she thought they did not want the labor of erecting the pavilion on this uneven ground, having just packed it tightly away.

She had left her little found statue by her side as she worked on the tapestry, and she picked it up now. Then as she turned to William she froze. Over his form she saw a shadowy figure.

God guide me, she thought as she peered through the darkness. The shape was too translucent to be mistaken for a wolf or other dangerous creature. Having first not spoken from surprise, she stayed silent now from caution. As she looked, the apparition took the form of a kind of grand lizard, and as William stirred, it echoed his movements. Finally she saw a flicker of its wings and glistening of scales. It was not beast that truly existed; it was a phantasm that her disbelieving eyes beheld.

With a start she dropped the ornament she still held, unthinking, in her hand—and as she did, the vision before her vanished. Finister appeared beside her, quite forgotten in the intervening period. She bent and retrieved the ornament and held it up to the light.

"A strange bauble," she said. "Oh, pardon, I mean no offense."

"Not at all," Margaret said. "It is just some trifle I found upon the road. I would not say it is pleasing to look at, but it seemed a pity to leave it by the roadside."

"Perhaps it is a good omen," Finister suggested as she set down the blankets under her arm and set to rolling them out, one on each side of where William lay. "'Tis the kings own sigil is it not, the dragon? And there is one with a harness upon it like a tame beast?"

"Yes, perhaps," Margaret mused as she turned the sinister little thing in her hand. "I don't think His Majesty would be any easier to tame than a dragon."

Finister laughed at what she took to be a joke, but Margaret barely manage a smile in reply.

She glanced very quickly to William to confirm that the odd vision was back but that all the others in their party still appeared quite ordinary, and then she dropped the wee dragon into her skirt pocket. Perhaps one of Harild's spies had planted it, but they could hardly know where she would go and that she would find it. What could it mean? She dared say nothing, despite her recent pledges, for fear or being taken for a witch. If she were wise, she would discard it quickly, for the most likely risk would be that it was found upon her and used as evidence for such a charge. But Margaret was not inclined to do this whilst yet uncertain of what the object was and how it came to her—it might yet prove some kind of advantage.

She went back to William's side and draped a throw over her shoulder as she slipped off her overdress. She set it to the side but as Finister came to collect it, she waved her away.

"Let it lie there," she said. "I may need it of...nature calls in the night."

Finister raised an eyebrow. "You might do better to wrap yourself in a blanket, but have it as you will."

Margaret put on hand out to William but he stiffened at her touch.

"Margaret," he said softly. "I've slept alone my whole life and I hope you understand if I ask you not be to close to me. It makes me uncomfortable."

Margaret felt her expression stiffen. How could she not feel affronted at such words? She was about to reply when Allen returned, probably from the call of nature himself. Margaret turned her back to William and lay down upon her side. What kind of man was he that even having her lie too near him was not allowable? It was as if he still thought she might attack him, or if he had a monkish distaste for a woman's flesh. If that were so, it did not bode well for their union although it made some sense of his recent words. Margaret lay still and mused gloomily upon what might yet prove to be a chaste marriage. She did not think herself a wanton, but that idea did not appeal to her. Margaret had not thought to control whom she married but she had hoped for a man not unpleasant to look at and willing—she had never aspired to be a nun.

Chapter Sixteen

"I have been inside too much recently," William insisted.

"But, William, you are not strong yet, and these are carriage horses, not riding hacks. They do not have smooth gaits or steady ways."

William clasped Allen by the shoulder. "You are my brother, not my mother. Credit me with the sense know my limits. I am sure someone will keep an eye on me... Finister, would you ride out this morning with me?"

"Of course, my lord," she readily agreed.

William was pleased at her compliance. She would surely be easy company and that, more than anything, was what he needed now.

"Then we are agreed," he said, as if saying it would make it so.

"If you insist, take my mare at least, she is meant for riding and schooled to it. I will take the carriage."

"Are you sure, Allen?" William joked. "Last time I borrowed her, I lost her, or she lost me."

Allen tried to smile but did not entirely succeed. "You might do better to keep Margaret company," he said. "She doesn't seem best pleased with you."

"In a little while, once I have taken the air a little and feel more like myself. It cannot be a good idea to attempt reconciliation in my current frame of mind."

Allen shook his head, but said no more as he left to assist in the hitching of the horses. Shandrick also looked less than pleased as he put Margaret's tack on one of the second pair of carriage horses, for Finister's use. William did his best to disregard their tempers; for all that he knew he would have to placate them later. Right now he just wanted to see the world from horseback, spreading in all direction rather than terminating on four stonewalls.

It took a while for everything to be packed and stowed, the horses hitched and the people ready to go. Shandrick and Berrick rode out in the lead upon the second carriage pair, matched bays with mouths of steel and hard gaits. Yarrow drove the carriage after them with Allen and Margaret inside. Finister and William followed.

"Allen instructed me most strictly to inform him if you look unwell," Finister said apologetically. Her first duty was obviously to her employer and master and William had no wish to make her uncomfortable.

"And so you must certainly do so," William replied. "I just hope that it will not be for some little while."

They ambled along behind the carriage as it struggled up the overgrown trial to the main road. There its wheels slipped into the dry ruts of the highway and its rumbling was quelled to a contented mutter. All about the green of summer was subsiding into the muted tones of winter. Bare branches showed in some placed where the leaves were beginning to fall. The air was fresh and dew sparkled in the fresh, early morning sun.

Finister kept her peace, as was a servant's habit unless addressed. William did not hold over-much with such formalities, but for the moment the silence suited him too much to break it.

"I rather think I need to apologize to Margaret," William finally said. "I don't think I am a terribly good husband."

"I suppose you learn it as you go," Finister said. "My late husband used to upset me without meaning to, but only in the beginning before he learned to understand my ways."

"I am sorry to hear that you lost him."

"Fever."

"Like my parents. I wish I knew why so people are taken so pointlessly..."

"We can only assume there is a reason for it, somehow."

William did not reply, he dare not for he had no such faith. They rode on, chatting of matters of no consequence as the morning deepened. The turned onto the White Road which would lead them all of the way to the Dragon Keep where the king of all Ordran held Summer Court.

At the intersection a dark cloaked man stood, holding the bridle of white mule. William stiffened to see him; from this distance the face was not distinguishable but the trailing, moth-eaten bearskin cloak was unmistakable. He gripped his reins and rode on, trying to give no sign of his disturbance. The other riders and the carriage passed Festrigan by and he did not hail them. William pulled his mare back and crossed behind Finister to pull up beside where Festrigan stood.

"No need for concern," Festrigan said. "I merely wish to tell you something. The very thing you asked me, before you left."

He seemed to speak the truth, but William took no particular chances and stayed mounted. Finister stayed close by his side, listening. William saw her meet Festrigan's challenging gaze but in the end the old man just shrugged.

"I thought you sought the Regent's Bridle, do you know what that is?"

Being an educated man, William had some small notion. "It is a myth, a royal myth, if not in its entirety then in the powers it claims."

"And they are?"

"It can tell who is king or should be, and um...something like ruling demons or fire."

"Not ruling them, letting them into the world. And it is not a myth. If you have it, I advise you to give it to me, for I have spent a lifetime researching this item and I of all men—possibly I alone—know the truth of the matter."

"For a man who knows the truth, you have some misconceptions," William replied stiffly. "I know nothing more about the matter than a few faded myths, I have never seen this item nor even believed in its existence—I would probably not even know it if I saw it."

"Somebody has it, the auguries say it has moved, that it is moving along this way."

"Then they may have it with my blessing, for I am not interested in witches or their tools."

William nudged his horse into motion, and Finister followed behind him.

"It has the shape of a dragon, William. A gold dragon. If you see it, bring it to me, bring it to me if you value your soul and those of all men."

They traveled down the road at an ambling walk, slowly gaining on the carriage. William could see Yarrow twisting in his seat to check on them, but turning back to his task as he saw them gaining.

"I think that man is mad," William mattered. "A magical gold dragon that would open a door to hell, can you imagine such a thing?"

It had been meant as a rhetorical question, but Finister answered with a quiet, "No indeed."

William reined his horse to a sudden halt. The lie stabbed at him like a nail driven into his temple by a deft carpenter. Finister went on a little, and had to wheel to come back to his side.

"Are you all right, Sir William? Shall I call Allen?"

"You've seen it, haven't you, this thing?"

Her eyes widened. "I don't know what you mean."

William's brow creased as the pain returned but he was braced for it this time. "It is pointless to lie to me, Finister. So unless you betray your master, Allen, in answering me I want you to tell me what you know."

Finister prevaricated but a short time. "It may be nothing," she said. "I only saw your wife with a trifle, a small object in the shape of a dragon. She keeps it by her in the pocket of her dress. But she seems to place not particular importance on it. I...I should say no more, for you can ask her yourself."

"Thank you, I shall."

William continued on his way, and Finister with him, this time in a more persistent silence.

They paused at noon beneath the shade of a grove of trees in the middle of a long shallow of land mostly filled marsh and briny swamp. William felt flat and confused. He could think of no good reason for Margaret to have this mythical object, nor could he convince himself of the coincidence. Dragons were ominous beasts not lightly depicted. They symbolized kingship in both its benevolent and terrible aspects. The dragon was an omen of sterility and war, as much as of strength and leadership. One did not simply make a trifle in the shape of such a beast—not wisely anyway for it would certainly attract ill luck.

His thoughts of apology to Margaret were swamped by his new doubts. He stood a little apart from the others after he settled his borrowed mount. His feet then took him to the highest vantage such as it was, a low mound almost completely encircled by the old trees. A single fallen tree provided a view across fallow land and directly down the road as it bent along the coast and disappeared between the Pently Hills on the way to the rich farmland of Arinbarrel.

He wondered if his wife were sent to him as an innocent, but her knowledge to be capitalized upon on her return, or even if she was to be used as hostage on the assumption he'd come to love her by this time. And yet as Margaret said, the king had no way of knowing she was here, and she had spoken truth in saying that.

William startled to hear a footstep amidst the dry leaves and he spun to see Allen had followed him.

"Your wife is good company," Allen said. "Perhaps you should discover that for yourself."

"She cannot be good company to one incapable of being good company," he snapped in return.

"Does your head hurt you?" Allen retorted. "If so then you should say rather than take it out on us. I can understand that a horse's motion is easier in such straights than a carriage's, which feels every lump in the ground. But rather than ride mayhap you should rest further and we should go on tomorrow. It is dry ground here with fresh water by, and we could camp."

"Nay, I'm just in a mood and can go on... As for Margaret, well, maybe I'm just not meant for finer feelings, Allen."

William meant to say, "I've never loved"—but what he heard himself say was this, "I've never loved but once."

"But once," Allen seized upon the phrase. "And when was that?"

William turned away, but Allen would not be shaken and came beside him, looking also down the White Road. "Are we leaving behind this pledge of honesty so soon, brother?" he asked sharply.

"What good does it do to love, where love does no good?" William replied.

"You speak in riddles, and you vex me."

"I cause many moods in you, and you in me. But imagine one thing that might yet cause your righteous brother to disown you, and what might it be, Allen?"

"My brother's narrow morals do not rule me."

"Your fortune and your fate depend upon his indulgence. As your friend, I know this. You should not risk calamity but for a prize that is worth the gamble."

William turned and walked back towards the carriage, where Yarrow and Shandrick watered the horses from buckets, as the sides of the stream were too steep to lead them to. Allen scrambled after him.

"William," he hissed. "We are not done with speaking. Not on this matter."

"Oh, but we are," William said firmly as he continued.

He sought out Margaret then, mainly to throw Allen off. All the while he wondered at his words. They spoke a truth he'd long known in some way, but never thought of so baldy. He loved Allen, not just as a foster brother, yet never properly as anything more than that. Much of the reason was cowardice on his part, but also caution for Allen's own precarious position. As a second son, he depended so entirely upon his dour brother's indulgence.

As he drew close, he saw Margaret sitting upon the carriage footboard. All he wanted was to know if she had this thing, this Regent's bridle. She looked up at him and her expression wavered.

"Forgiven me yet?" William said.

"Forgiven you?"

William leaned against the side of the carriage. "For being scared of you. Scared of any woman, or man for that matter, when it comes to being too close. You only need ask Allen about that. I don't know if I'll ever...well."

Margaret's expression softened. "You can hardly be..."

"When it comes to women; I think you'll find I can."

Margaret glanced around. "You can't mean that you're..."

"No need to be coy, a virgin. I am. If I'd been born to different parents, I don't doubt that I'd be a monk. I think that would have suited me."

Margaret stood and took his hand. "Come walk with me awhile," she said.

"Perhaps..."

"Shh, they'll manage."

She drew him away, down along the side of the small stream where the grass grew long and great tufts of seed heads reached up over their heads. William was very conscious of his hand being held—a slight dampness where skin touched skin. She took them some few minutes walk away across the soggy ground. Finally she stopped and turned to him, squaring him to her with a hand on each forearm.

"We could have some practical arrangement, many couples do. But maybe we don't have to settle for that. I want you to do something for me."

She took one step in towards him and drew his arms to encircle her. Part of William's mind was on the item in her skirt pocket, but not entirely. His hands rested on her waist, slipping a little lower from there. Beneath the starch cloth of her dress, he felt the soft warmth of her body.

William's heart had barely recognized it loved a man, his body knew immediately what it felt about a woman. The heat was there in his loins. He shifted his feet awkwardly, not wanting to give himself away to a woman he had resolved to cede to another.

Margaret's fingers curled around his arms, stroking up towards his shoulders. She looked him directly in the eyes, having to tilt her chin up given his extra height. William looked to the side and down to the ground, his breath feeling loud and shallow, catching in his throat.

"Tell me, William, what do you feel?"

This was a moment when a lie would be very handy, though if she stood just a little closer, she would know some part of the truth regardless. Maybe he could love her, and she him, and she could be damned with him. But what could he say to turn her away from him, for he didn't have the heart to hurt her—nor knew any truth that would serve.

"I didn't want to marry," he said softly.

"Do you want to be married to me now?"

"Please understand when I say, it would be better if we were not..."

He felt her spine stiffened at the words and he could not stop himself from adding a softening caveat. "I am in trouble, I can feel it, and I fear to drag down another with me. I should not have married you."

"But you did, is it so terrible?"

She leaned into him and William's hands moved of their own volition to splay across her shoulders, sliding down to curl around her waist.

"I think it would be best to have some chance of freeing you from this marriage," he forced out each word with distinct effort. "It is not consummated, it is not irreversible."

"William," her voice was muffled against his chest, "you think the worst when so little is known for sure. Hold onto me. Hold onto me and we will get through this. So if the king has gone mad and has some campaign against us—we will go somewhere else. Together."

He pushed her away slowly, his desire for her surely no secret, as close as she had stood to him.

"Go away as some penniless gypsy. I'd not do that to you."

"It is my choice. I would choose it because I combined my fate with yours and I chose to honor that. I..."

"It is not entirely your choice," William interrupted. "You cannot be wife to a man who will not be husband. You are a noblewoman, not a beggar. Your life is in a court or keep, not tilling some dusty field or begging by a roadside."

Imagining her in such straits made it easier for William to refuse her, but she only grew angrier in return.

"So why did you marry me? No. You may tell yourself these things but the real reason is different. You have not forgiven me."

"Forgiven you for... No, truly..."

"I was not faithful. One lonely occasion and God had already punished me for that. He took the child, the child who was never meant to be."

Margaret's voice choked as anger dissolved into grief. William tried to step away, to leave her, but could not. He went back to her with his arms outstretched.

"No, Margaret, truly. We made a bad start and I am sure it was just somehow not meant to be. The child, I should have said. I am sorry, Margaret." William felt tears in his eyes as he said it. "I am sorry about the child, despite everything it was—I feel responsible."

"How could you be responsible, William dear?"

William knew too well he was entirely at fault, but could do no more than shrug. "We must, I suppose, move on from here as best we may. But I do fear getting too close to you and I have a premonition that it would not be best for you. It is not, perhaps, entirely a rational thing but it is an imperative that I feel. That I should not...be with you. That this is not meant to happen."

"William, William."

She clearly did not know what to say, and in truth, his words could not be making very much sense to her.

"'Tis foolish sounding, I don't doubt," he said. "But it is what I think and what I feel."

"And I feel otherwise and must convince you."

William greatly feared that he heard a stubbornness in her voice to match his own, but on this occasion all she did was offer a hand, that they might return to the others, together.

Chapter Seventeen

Harild stretched out his long legs and heard his stiff ankle pop in protest. He had sat through an interminable meeting with his financial counselors and was less than pleased to find he had another meeting scheduled with one of Serle's lackeys. His heart felt dull and he wondered how it was that being king has become such a tedious occupation. It was little more than a procession of routine tasks and audiences with men who wanted something he could give but had little to offer in return. No doubt this was another of these.

The old earl was one of his staunchest supporters, but foisting this old bird on him might well be stretching the matter. Harild glared at this stooped specimen and mentally promised that he'd regret it if he didn't have something damned interesting to say for himself.

"So, you have the private audience you asked for," Harild said in a tone that hovered just short of gracious. "I suggest that you justify your need for this indulgence as I have many things I would rather be doing this moment."

It was only Serle's name that gained this man such privileged access. Harild was mindful of the earl's role in securing his throne, and his recent message updating his knowledge as to William's whereabouts. Serle's message had been rather cryptic though, saying not only that he held William but that he hesitated to release him, as he might "know something of importance to the crown". The "crown" rather than the "king" was an aside that suggested Serle might know that Harild was not king Parlon's son. But that knowledge was hardly rare, and of little use to a man who could not prove it. If only he dared make himself more clear, but messengers were easily bribed and things set down on paper might end up anywhere. Harild could only assume that it was no great matter, or the earl would have traveled to court himself to seek his king's counsel.

"I do apologize," the old commoner said. "But this will take some telling. If you bear will me, you will see why I felt driven to inconvenience Your Royal Highness with my presence at this time."

Harild's pursed his lips, but he resolved to give this man a hearing. He leaned back and folded his arms, thinking wistfully of the ride he had meant to take—he had not been out of the keep these past ten days and might not for some time to come. There was said to be a fine stag in the dell by the old chapel, and Harild did not want some damned poacher to take it before he had the chance. The old man awaited permission to continue and with a scowl, Harild rallied his attention to this audience, and gave it.

"The Regent's Bridle has been lost some eighty years, since the time of your great-grandfather. Most of this time, it has been somewhere in the fields surrounding the highway of Ghent, just off the northern most extremity of the White Road. Recently it was uplifted from that place and taken down the White Road and in the direction of this very household."

Harild's weary tolerance was transformed immediately. He had continued to promulgate the notion that the Bridle's powers were just a myth, all the time knowing that this was not true. The Bridle, in the hands of a descendent of Lukas, would open the gate into the world of dragons. Harild's heart began to beat faster as he contemplated the possibility of holding the Bridle in his hands with great magical beasts bowing down cravenly before him. To return the dragons, to command the dragons. Having them back in the world would transform him from the ruler of a faded rump of formerly grand empire to a true king of Ordran, to a king of Ordran and it territories again—taking back those upstart islands and all these surrounding lands that had drifted from his grandfather's grasp.

"You knew where it was," he said coolly as if it was not news to him, merely something he'd not wanted widely known.

In truth, the fact outraged him, for he had not, and the Bridle was by its very nature the property of the royal line of Ordran. It was of very little use in the hands of any other man. He craved possession of the Bridle as other men might want women or drink, but he dared not speak widely of it for fear of sparking other men's interests and motivating their own searches for this immensely powerful device. Yet Harild was willing to forgive much given that this man brought him the kind of news that promised to banish his boredom for some time to come.

Festrigan raised his hands beseechingly. "I informed the earl and left to him to say more, whilst I tried to locate it exactly on your behalf. I have no doubt that you understand the might of this item and the absolute necessity of Bridle being kept safe—that it not be employed. We—I mean you, Your Highness, with my assistance only to the extent you command it—must seize the Bridle before this man employs it. He might at any moment bring about incomparable calamity."

Harild's face showed nothing of his amazement. Not employed? There was obviously some great disparity between his knowledge of the Bridle's powers and this ragged scholar's, but given that Harild had access to the first inscribed records of the gifting of the Bridle from Garwolf Nightwing to Lukas the First of Ordran, he had no doubt that his comprehension was the sounder of the two. After all, Festrigan did not even seem to know that the Bridle worked only in conjunction with the gate, the Dragon Gate that lay long undisturbed in a cavern beneath the keep.

But he was inclined to be cautious, this Festrigan knew enough to be dangerous on the matter—and that was a rare thing. Maybe even rare enough to be useful, if properly handled.

Harild still ruled for two reasons. Firstly, he moved swiftly and sure when he saw the need, and secondly he did little but watch and wait whilst matters were unclear. At this moment he employed the later, precautionary principle. He merely nodded in a way that might be taken to imply agreement and leaned back into his leather-slung chair. "Go on," he said. "I would hear what you have to say."

Festrigan wrung his hands as he paced before the king as if delivering a lecture to a row of school children. "I do not know who exactly has the Bridle, but I suspect. I suspect Sir William of White Lady Tor. Serle had him in custody and most unwisely released him..."

Harild raised his hand and interrupted perfunctorily. "The earl was instructed by me to, as it is my wish that William come here to me."

He saw Festrigan wondering just how much the king knew already. The old scholar was obvious a most disingenuous man, and he would not part with more information then he felt he had to establish some foothold of influence. But currently he seemed confused, a state Harild greatly preferred to foster in all who were not his most trusted confidants. In truth, he had known nothing at all about the Bridle's involvement the current state of affairs—he had long assumed it to be lost or even destroyed.

"My apologies," Festrigan stuttered belatedly. "You are, of course, wise to take charge of this matter. I only wish to lay before you any facts in my possession that might aid you."

Harild did not believe that statement to be in the least sincere. He suspected the scholar wished to get his own hands on the Bridle, but he did not yet know why. Perhaps it was just that he was entranced with it, as scholars sometimes were with some great thing they studied—it sparked a kind of avarice not known to man with broader and more natural habits. To get the information he needed without giving anything away the king knew that he needed to do no more than keep his silence.

Festrigan fixed Harild with a presumptuously stone-faced and inquisitorial stare. "I am sure we both know that there are many who wish to bring demons back into our world, and I believe William...."

"Sir William," Harild interrupted, mainly to keep the old scholar off-balance and let him know that he should not assume William was of no consequence.

"Excuse me, Sir William, to be one of these. That he uses the art of magic is quite clear to me. His ability to influence the earl, and other factors around him suggest that he is in the service of the devil. Indeed, when confronted about this by both myself and my lord Serle, he conspicuously refused to deny it."

"A follower of the devil who will not lie?" Harild asked with raised brows.

"He seems in many ways an honest man, but he is driven and in some form of pact perhaps with his fellow knight Allen of Argent and even, I think, his wife."

Harild's patience was beginning to fray. He did not know Lady Margaret well, but he knew *of* her quite well from her mother, who was a friend of long-standing although no longer his lover. If ever there was a woman not likely to sell her soul, it was Margaret. She was forthright at times but too good-natured to become troublesome. Festrigan seemed to sense that he was losing his audience but was wise enough not to interrupt Harild's musings.

Harild turned his thoughts to Allen, an able knight but light of mind and morals. No. If there were any man driving the matter is would be William. Harild was not so superstitious as to believe tales of the devil, of mistake a dragon for a demon even all these years after the last dragon had faded from the world.

"Sir William is being directed in his actions, perhaps even coerced," Festrigan said. "I spoke to him at length and his education is not arcane, his interests are not in the sphere of the soul and its salvation. I know he bears the Bridle, but I am convinced that he does not do so for himself. There is a higher power at work through him, and this being, great demon or as I suspect the devil, may have taken one of the others as his primary disciple. The Bridle must be seized from him, before it is too late."

Harild played for a little time to think by standing and going to his side table where a decanter of sweet wine stood by a single goblet. He poured a small measure, offering none to his guest. It was not his habit to encourage petitioners to linger. There was one question he desperately wanted to ask, but he also wanted it to sound like nothing more than an idle query.

"Well, in your assessment, what sort of man is Sir William? He is but a minor knight and do not believe that I recall him."

Festrigan was openly pleased to have his opinion sought. "I am told he fights well," he said. "He has taken an injury to his head and so I may not be hest able to judge his character. We spoke over several hours in several days and my assessment is that he is serious for one so young, but needs to be watched. He is cautious and willful—the kind of man who might take it into his head to do most anything, and give no warning before 'tis done."

Harild had to suppress a smile. Some years past that might well have served as a description of himself, and it delighted him beyond measure to hear it. He had been most careful to distance himself from Katinka's child; for all that he had been in her belly long before her elopement with his old and former friend Garreth of the Tor. A true son of Garreth would have been an altogether more obvious and fiery-tempered boy...

With time he had come to see some advantage to her betrayal of his trust, she took a child, most likely his child, into hiding. And as the years had never brought a proper heir, it had pleased him to have this man, most likely his son, kept secret, in reserve. Harild's more fickle and younger followers began to sway from him, fearing the loss of their privileges when he died and some other man with followers of his own took the throne. Certainly there was no shortage of contenders, their avaricious ranks swelling every day and thwarting each other in their jostling for position. It was only a matter of time before one of the more foolish chose to hasten him on his way to death. It was a situation that did not please Harild and that pleased him less every day. To name an heir might not quell them, for a named heir might yet be challenged—but to name an heir who was his son, that would be enough to silence all but the most reckless of challengers.

Now that dissent was stirring, he had known he might need to learn more of William and acknowledge him. This is why he had sent his former mistress' daughter—barring a two-year gestation she was by no means his own—to be William's wife. It blocked any other from gaining William's favor by the offer of a better dowered match, it also put by him a women sound of heart and quick enough of mind to serve him well, not one inevitably spurred by ambition—as would be the case once the boy's paternity was named.

"I thank you for coming this long way to tell me this most important news," Harild said evenly. "You will take lodging here in the keep whilst I look into the matter. I would have your advanced understanding of the issues at my disposal, if it pleases you."

That last was mostly rhetorical, but the flattery implied would be enough to sweeten the old man into compliance. Festrigan bowed agreement and backed towards the door. Harild watched him leave with satisfaction. He'd brought interesting news after all. To have a son to name was good, to have one who showed such initiative was very fine. Harild did not doubt that he could bring his son to heel. Regardless of his native talents he had not the experience his father had hard won. That it might be a slight challenge only fired Harild's blood and made him anticipate the coming days, as he had not since the time of his ascendancy.

His wife, the so-called queen, would see her place and that of her insipid daughters soon displaced. Harild greatly anticipated the arrival of his son. Somehow he felt quite certain William was his son although a man can never entirely be sure. Well, he would know on seeing the lad. He had high hopes for him, for who but his son would seize the opportunity the Bridle presented, who but his son was be distinguished by his skill in his very first real battle?

Harild's smiled in premature paternal pride, anticipating the arrival of his heir. Surely it would be a simple matter, for the deal he had to offer was a fine one. Mayhap William already knew most of the facts and was well on his way to make the same deal—to swap a magical bauble for a royal inheritance.

Once that was accomplished, Harild would have it all. He would be king of men, and king of dragons, with a son to inherit both of those crowns. His heart swelled to imagine it. Harild had been born with a king's nature but not yet proved to be a great one—a fact of which he was painfully aware. He wanted to be remembered like Lukas was, not so much as a man but as a blessed king, revered as almost an angel of God. He wondered idly how long a dragon lived, perhaps old Garwolf was still around, still bound to the agreement he had made.

Dragons who entered the world of men must be obedient to a man of Lukas's blood who held the Bridle. Men who entered the dragon's world were likewise ruled. There were enough curious individuals from either race to make this an interesting bargain. Dragon were great and bore with them magic that those around them might employ—what the dragons did with men Harild did not know nor did he care. All he knew for sure was that no man or dragon who crossed could ever return. It was a form of exile intrinsic to the magic of the gate—anyone fickle enough to leave was not allow any opportunity to return. They went to be little more that a servant of another race.

For all his grand imaginings, nothing was sure as yet. But surely if the boy had inherited his father's sense, he was see that it was no bad deal to swap a magical bauble for the inheritance of the same, with the whole kingdom of Ordran thrown in to boot.

Harild idled awhile trying to imagine what a dragon might look like, but more than that, what it must be like to have such creatures at your command. He roused himself from such pleasant contemplation and rang the bell for his manservant. He had much to do in preparation. He must put William in the right rooms to observe him, but ones too distant to draw the attention of others. He would need to send an escort to keep the boy company on the road, but not one that would be too obvious. He must keep the queen in ignorance by finding some other intrigue to distract her spies and draw away her meddling influence. He must by all means keep William from getting into the deep room beneath the keep where the dormant gate still lay, bereft of its only key. And, finally, would have to speak with William without giving any of his plans away away. Indeed, he must continue to seem begrudging of Garreth's son as if pursuing their feud beyond the grave.

He started to call for servants and followers to do his wishes.

Chapter Eighteen

"The king, it seems, couldn't be less interested in your William, and you know what that means?" Aunty Medry leaned into Margaret, her breath thick with mint tea and sherry. "It means the old fox is very interested indeed."

She leaned back with a matter-of-fact nod and picked her tapestry frame up from her ample lap. It was a gesture that suggested she had imparted the bulk of the news that she had for Margaret. Margaret was tired from traveling but fought to understand, to defend her husband from any who might conspire against him.

"But I do not know what he has done to draw the king's attention?" she ventured.

Medry was an old friend of Margaret's mother, and a long-serving servant to the royal family—wet-nurse to the king's eldest daughter and nanny to the youngest child. It was a fine balance of loyalties but Margaret was only giving her a chance to talk, not pressuring her to do so. Fortunately Medry chose to speak on.

"There is chatter, you know, just gossip. They say that there might have been more than one birth that happened a little off its proper time. His mother being a royal mistress you know. Of course it puts an end to one rumor."

Margaret fiddled with her teacup and tried to untangle exactly what Medry was trying to convey to her. A woman of court was not expected to need things spelled out to her—a birth out of time, Katinka's child perhaps being...the king's. Margaret felt a cool wave pass through her body. "More than one rumor?"

"Oh, child. Even the old fox wouldn't have wed you to your brother. For all that they'd not say a word to you about it directly—you will have to look elsewhere than the king for a father. Which is no tragedy as I see it. Royal blood at one step removed or the wrong side of the blanket can be a good enough advantage—but you don't want to be in spitting distance of the throne, my girl, it's like setting up home in the cemetery. But do tell me how is the old man's offspring, eh?"

"Oh." Margaret tried to look unflustered but she could feel a blush in her cheeks. The very fact she was getting gossip from Medry suggested that she was not one to impart personal secrets to. "I could have done a lot worse than William," she said coyly.

She was not looking forward to imparting this news to William. For all that he was properly loyal, William had no love for the king. He did not enjoy intrigues, nor did he aspire to anything more than to be a knight and firm his grasp on the lands of the Tor and their accompanying titles. To find that he might be the king's son, it would not please him at all.

৩৯

"You are too modest," Lord Yarmoth proclaimed, slapping William heartily on the back and propelling him forward onto the table. "My boy remembered quite clearly that you charged in just as some bastard was about to run him through with a pike. Another drink here, and all around."

That was an easy order to make, as it was the king's hospitality he offered. Yarmoth pressed another brimming tankard into William's hand. It was only afternoon but the hall was already full of men making free with the king's food and drink. The recent battle was very much the topic of the day, and growing with each telling. William had only been trying to find where Allen had been lodged but Yarmoth had intercepted him. And there was no gracious way to escape, a knight was expected to hold his own in carousing as well as fighting.

William tried to look at ease with the other men crowded around the long table, and hoped he would not be stuck in their company 'til nightfall. Still they insisted on hearing some accounts of the action from him, and imparting some of their own. Time wore on, but custom did not allow William to leave whilst the others stayed and made him welcome.

"Mixed luck to be captured," Yarmoth said. "Damned inconvenient I'm sure, but it means you fought on the day they triumphed and not the day they lost, eh?"

William couldn't really take that as a joke. "I'd rather have been there," he replied sourly.

"Of course you would, old Frank said you almost had his neck, and that it took two of them to get you."

William wondered if "Frank" had said more than that, but Yarmoth drifted onto other topics. Mainly the action of the first day again, which William did not recall with any detail. They seemed content to pore over every detail, and at inexorable length. William merely smiled and agreed with anything the older knight proposed, trying to drink as slowly as he might without seeming callow as they refilled his cup whenever its level dropped and the cup was never empty. It was with some relief that he saw Allen coming towards him.

"Of course if Sir Allen had not provided a mount I would have been in dire straits," William said in the hopes of deflecting their attention.

"I see you have cornered my precocious brother," Allen said, leaning in to refill William's cup. "Drink up, and then hurry off. He's just recently married, you know."

The others shouted at him to drink and William drained his cup, not sure how many that made if you added up each part-portion poured from the jug. He was glad for Allen providing an excuse to leave, no matter how bawdy, and to have finally found his old friend—or at least be found by him. William got to his feet, albeit unsteadily. He reached out to keep himself upright and Allen caught him. The others called after them, suggestions and jokes best not heeded closely.

"Where have you been, Allen? I was looking for you." William could hear the slur in his own voice but he could not control it.

"Not very hard I would say. I am in the euphemistically named bachelor's quarters. In all honesty, the stables look more snug... Watch yourself here."

They managed to traverse the hall and turn into one of the many passages from the antechamber beyond. Partway along there was a narrow stair that led to his and Margaret's room. William missed the step and would have fallen had Allen not caught him about the waist.

"Not so precocious with your drink at least," Allen said as he helped William clamber up the narrow coils of stone steps more fitting for a servant's stair than a main passageway. The small access pressed them close together and Allen was obviously holding him tight lest he fall in this steep and dangerous place.

Allen's face was very close to his, so that he could feel his warm breath. William was struck but a clutching feeling in his chest and a deep and sudden desire to kiss William. They were alone in a narrow, spiral stair, surround by nothing but the curves of the stone. Suddenly there was nothing more in the world that he wanted to do then feel Allen's flesh against his own, and only the most slender thread of doubt held him back from it. He thought that Allen sensed it, and that might make all of the difference. How long had Allen waited for this tacit permission and how would he refuse it?

But Allen stepped back bashfully. "Best get you back to your rooms them, at the end here I think?"

William's befuddled mind groped in the darkness for something it seemed to have lost. Allen all but dragged him up the stair and along the hall to their small room in an inauspicious but central cul-de-sac of the keep. He opened the door and propelled him cheerfully forward. "Here he is, my dear, mystery solved."

He then beat a hasty retreat, leaving William swaying in the center of the room as Margaret stood from a chair by the fireplace. Having spent most of his life quite sure it would be improper to lie with a man, he had to admit to feeling aggrieved at losing this belated opportunity. In the morning when he was sober he was sure he would think better of it, but as it was, he wished he could run after Allen.

"Allen..." Margaret began, but the click of the door being pulled closed suggested there were little point in continuing.

"There was...um. Some celebrations," William said vaguely. "I got a little sidetracked."

He stared at the single canopy bed that dominated the room. Margaret came up to him. "Best you sleep it off, I think," she said.

Margaret stepped up to him and unbuckled his belt, as if it were the most natural act in the world. She tugged up his tunic, over his had. William felt extremely vulnerable as the cloth covered his eyes and his almost-wife stood before his bare chest.

He pulled the thick tunic off, down his arms. "I am sure I can manage..."

"Oh hush," she said, taking it from him. "I am only folding your clothes. And that done, you'll get in that bed and in a little while I'll join you there. I'll not have talk about us even if it is true. So choose which side you want and I'll not bother you."

William smiled weakly. Now with his functions muted with drink, his lower instincts stirred, he felt them under fragile rein as she stood before him. Having vowed to touch neither Allen nor Margaret, he had already failed one and would take little prompting to fail again and more completely. He stood a long while looking across at her and then not trusting himself to speak she turned away. William backed away towards the bed. He felt something for Margaret, if he was honest with himself, and had come to know her a little, respect a great deal, and recently...desire her.

He cursed his wayward lusts. How could he get his good friends together whilst he wanted to bed each in turn when the opportunity presented itself? William chided himself and struggled to keep his purpose in mind. Surely these impulses were devil-sent and should not be indulged.

William sat on the side of the bed and, with some difficulty, pulled off his boots and pulled of his trews. He looked over with ridiculous bashfulness to see if Margaret was watching him before pulling off his drawers and slipping under the cool, heavy covers. Margaret seemed to be occupied in folding his clothes and setting them upon the window seat. She then lit two candles and set them on the mantle beside her as if she meant to stay up a while longer. That was a mercy, at least, for if she had come to him, William felt sure he would not have refused her no matter what he resolved.

§·

Margaret was beginning to despise her embroidery. The White Lady stood at its center, her feet planted upon distinct, hump-backed outcropping of the Tor, with the castle shown, a little out of proportion, at its base. It was said that the White Lady was an elf who came from the underhill to marry a mortal knight. One day the elves discovered that the way into the world of men was going to close, and they all made haste to return to their own land before it was too late. All except the White Lady, who remained with her husband. But when the gate closed and the elven magics left the word she wasted away and died.

Margaret wondered what that story was meant to suggest, that a wife should be faithful and cleave always to her husband, or that a pragmatic woman would realize there were limits to such faithfulness? After all, if her husband had loved her wouldn't he want her to live, even if it was far from him? Perhaps it was just a tragedy, meant to tug at the heartstrings by showing how even the most virtuous might win only a life that was painful and short.

It would be better if she had some beads to highlight the hem of her dress and pick out her headdress, and it was annoying that she had not brought more green thread. Of course she could borrow some here but being from a different lot the colors would not properly match.

All of these thoughts were just a screen behind which Margaret's real feelings hid. She saw William slide his long legs under the bedclothes. Seeing his body, even so covertly, has a strange effect on her. His was a lean form, each side matched as if by a mirror, and of a slightly swarthy tone of skin. There were icons of angels in the church that would suffer by comparison except that this was not distant, immaculate spirit but a body of palpable softness and warmth.

Margaret sensed the weakening of William's will to deny her, but on several counts she hesitated. Firstly she would not want him to think she connived to win him by stealth or unfair advantage. She wanted him to come to her as much as she went to him. Honesty seemed important to him for all that he kept his teeth clamped closed over so many matters.

Then there was the matter of their confused paternity. Could she be sure the king would not marry a man to his half-sister? Harild might well be William's father and fear the bastard child would threaten the inheritance of his daughters— an incestuous marriage once revealed would stop William from ever ascending to a righteous throne. The very thought of it made Margaret shudder, but if that was the king's motive, it was a thing that he might do. Could she really be thinking as she had about her brother?

Finally there was the damned dragon-thing. She slipped it from her pocket and held it in her hand, concealed from sight by her embroidery. She turned to the bed and between the pulled back canopy drapes she saw the creature spelled out in shifting smoke, a dragon curled in slumber. Did it mean her husband was some kind of creature? Or was she just being drawn into witchcraft by a cursed object—something she just could not make herself cast aside.

It was then that the thought struck her, the sigil of Lukas's line was a dragon. Perhaps it was simply trying to tell her something, to tell her that William descended from the dragon king. Margaret wished she had more experience of magic. She stood very quietly and went to stand before the burnished mirror, but she saw only her own dim refection.

She needed to take counsel, and with her mother passed away, there were few she could turn to. She felt two conflicting instincts. One was to slip into the bed beside her husband; the other was to speak to her most constant supporter, Allen of Argent. She crept over to William, his head lay lax upon the pillow and his breath was slow. Even as she watched, his eyes flickered under their lids in a way that happened only during true sleep.

In many ways, Margaret knew her actions were risky, but she donned her cloak and stepped out into the dark hall. Allen had pointed out his rooms to her from the vantage of the window. She found her way out into the small garden court that separated them. She knew better than to go inside the building where her presence would certainly be noticed.

His window was on the ground floor and light showed between the slats of the closed shutters. Margaret rapped lightly on the outside and heard somebody stirring inside. She prayed that Allen was alone in there or some embarrassment might follow, but she would not make it worse by trying to hide until she saw him.

The shutters swung out and Allen stood there wearing only a crumpled robe.

"Margaret," he said. "You should not be here, have you no sense?"

"There is something I must speak to you in private about."

"Not at night, and through a window. We shall sit in the garden here tomorrow after breakfast, openly and with no appearance of deceit. I will not have it said that I am acting to you other than I should."

Margaret wavered, but belatedly realized that he was right. If they spoke openly and without embarrassment, it would not be looked at askance. But before that time she held what might be a cursed item in her hands and slept beside a man who might be her brother but who drew her almost like no other. Like no other, bar one. Margaret saw the danger then, not only in the appearance of infidelity but the possibility of it. Allen stood before her, his hair unkempt and robe gaping to show an expanse of pale flesh.

Margaret backed away. "You are wise, I'm sure, I'm sorry. Until tomorrow."

"Not at all. I'll be there."

He did not draw the shutters closed but watched until she went back inside through the small garden door. Margaret went back up the stairs and into their room. William seemed to have slept on and not missed her.

Margaret looked down at him and held the golden dragon. The translucent dragon also dozed and Margaret reached out one hand, but felt nothing as it passed through that illusory surface.

The person she should speak to was William. In the morning, she should do as he asked and tell him all she knew. Then they might go and meet Allen together. It would not be any easy thing to do, but Margaret did not want to be like so many wives always scheming not only for their husbands but against them.

She slipped off her dress and laid it over a chair back with the dragon ornament within its pocket again. She blew out the candles and slipped into the cool far side of the bed. In the darkness, she was acutely conscious of William lying so closely by, but it was an image of Allen at the window that flashed through her mind's eye. No matter how she commanded her heart to seek her husband out, it seemed to expand to embrace both of these, so different, men. Though she would be fortunate to win even the one she had, and should not allow herself to be distracted.

Chapter Nineteen

Ahriman lingered in the room, watching the couple sleep. The more time he spent around these apparently unremarkable mortals, the stranger he felt. It was almost as if he was becoming accustomed to their company. Although only William knew he was there, and he was hardly thrilled at the prospect. Odd, fragile things, these men and women were. Ahriman recalled catching William as he fell from the window at Serle's keep, a fragile body plummeting down onto the stones—it would have been so easy to let him fall and go to look for more amusing sports. Certainly he had done as much many time before when his chosen prey disappointed him. But in this case he was beginning to feel stirring of most uncharacteristic compassion. What could be the cause of that, surely not this gangly and callow knight?

He saw Margaret stir; she craned her neck to look at William who lay quiet but awake, staring up at the cobwebs on the underside of the bed canopy. This room was certainly not allotted to them to show that the king held them both as the apple of his eye. William and Margaret locked gazes in the dim confines of the heavily draped bed. There was a beginning of some kind of accord between them, although it was still fragile yet. She was also a very commonplace woman, but Ahriman could tell that she and William would suit each other well if only they were allowed to, not least by their own fears and doubts.

"Good morning, husband," Margaret said with thin cheer. Her tone deepened immediately as she broached the topic that had been on her mind most of the night. Neither of them had slept a great deal, but lain locked in their respected silences throughout the interminable night. "I said we might meet Allen in the garden after breakfast, but first there are two things that I have learned and must tell you. I have heeded what you said about honesty between we three, but these are things I think you should hear first. It is just that they are both difficult to say..."

William's expression was schooled to bland and open interest, but his body was tense. "Take what time you need. I promise you, I will never be angry with you if you tell the truth, not matter what it be."

Margaret slipped from the bed and went to where her dress hung, she clutched it before her, clad only in a thin shift. She twisted the cloth as she approached him like some child having to confess some small sin.

"But all the same, I do not enjoy bringing difficult news," she said. "But 'tis better known than not, surely. If there were a matter relating to you, you would want to know it?"

Ahriman knew that his purpose was better served by silence, yet he felt a sense of anticipation that was almost eager in its tone. It was interesting to see how these two danced around each other, but each for their own reasons, never quite coming together. It might even be interesting to see them in each other's arms. Now there was a peculiar thought. It might actually be interesting to see these two mortals happy. Surely there are as many shades to happiness as to grief, as many subtleties?

"Of course," William said. He reached out his arm to Margaret and she came to sit on his side of the bed. He put his arm awkwardly around her waist as he sat up to listen to her. The touch between them, outwardly so casual but there was a spark to it, like the promise of lightening.

"I spoke to an old family friend," she said. "And she tells me that there are rumors. They say that the king might be your father, your mother carrying you before she left the court."

William blinked and stared across the room. He did not believe it, but nor did he disbelieve it. It just sat like a stone upon his mind, as a possibility. Margaret knew how William treasured the memory of his mother and she dreaded how he might react. They were a quiet, frozen tableau as he waited to see what he actually did feel about it.

"We cannot know if the rumors are true," Margaret continued softly. "But I am concerned because many consider I might be his daughter and thus our marriage...improper."

William sighed and leaned back onto his pillow. "Improper would be a mild way of putting it. I suppose I must await his summons and put these matters to him then. I suppose it is another reason to be cautious...to realize our marriage may not be a marriage in truth. I mean..."

He looked over to Margaret and noted that she was still rigid with tension.

"What else is there?" he asked wearily. "Surely there cannot be to much more for us to deal with before the king makes his wishes known."

"This is, if anything, more important, and more difficult because I am not sure exactly what it is I am telling you. Perhaps it would be easier to show you."

187

She drew out the Bridle. It seemed so innocuous nestled in her palm, like some small trinket—perhaps a strangely shaped paperweight. In the dim light, William took a little while to see its shape clearly. It was somewhat rounded in its extremity, from decades of handling and wear. The details were marked out in tarnish and dirt. The little dragon seemed to leer, its minute teeth clamped over a comic carthorse's bit.

"Do you know what this is?" Margaret asked with a quaking voice.

"I do, do you?"

Margaret shook her head. "I found it on the road when we paused but briefly to change the horses. It had disturbed me ever since but I am ashamed to say I hesitated to tell you about it. I do not want you thinking me a witch. I hardly dare say what I see when I hold it. You do believe me, don't you, that I never sought it out, I just came upon it?"

"Oh aye, I do. May I?"

As well he might. Ahriman smiled. William was gradually coming to appreciate the value of the gift he had been given.

William reached for the Regent's bridle and as he took it a shiver ran through Ahriman. He felt something deep in his nature melt and change. It was a situation beyond disconcerting, that a simple man's actions should so affect him. Something was very amiss in this business, something even he was not aware of. Ahriman peered at them both, remaining quite invisible. Perhaps it was just the influence of the Regent's Bridle. It was a powerful object and he might be wise to remove it now. But Ahriman could not make himself do it. Part of him had to recognize that it seemed fitting that William had it, like it was meant to be. Like all of this somehow rotated around bringing the Bridle into William's hands—and feeling so peripheral to matters was not a sensation Ahriman enjoyed.

William held the Bridle and examined it a long time. He put it down on the bedcover and reached for his trousers. Margaret looked coyly away as he dressed, and perhaps to cover his own embarrassment he spoke to her as he did so. The Bridle lay upon the bedcover and Ahriman itched to pick it up and bear it away to the anonymous field where it had lain so long.

"I have been told by one of Serle's followers that there is an item, shaped like a dragon, and those who hold it can tell who carries the blood of the first king. And more than that, one who has that blood may use the Bridle to open a door into a world of demons and let them into this world. But, Margaret, I do have my doubts about this account. 'Tis in the shape of a dragon, and Lukas was called the Dragon King. I have pondered on it and I wonder if the myths about the Lukas are true."

"The myths?" Margaret asked.

William straightened his tunic and turned to her. "That there were dragons then and he commanded them. That there really were dragons and they made Ordran a great land, feared and admired by all."

Margaret shook her head. "Dragons? It seems no more likely than the tales elves or unicorns."

William raised his hand. "But if you think on it, the tales speak of a way opening between the worlds and beings of fantastic races entering into ours, or sometimes humans going into theirs. When the way is open they can come here, and bring something of their world with them, like magic. But when the way closes, they must return or linger and die."

"Like the White Lady."

"Like the White Lady. Perhaps 'tis just a myth, but if it is not, how would we know? If the distant past truly was more magical and there were creatures, marvelous creatures, what if that is what this thing does? Let in the dragons."

"Dragons," Margaret echoed softly. "Would that be so much better? Are they not enormous ravening beasts? Demons or dragon I think it must be better for the gate to be left closed. But...Pick it up," Margaret said, "and look at me. What do you see."?

William looked like he would have liked an explanation first, but he did not demand one. He picked up the little dragon and watched her levelly for some time. "I see nothing unusual," he said quizzically. "What did you expect?"

Margaret went over to the wall and lifted the heavy metal mirror from its pegs. She brought it over, holding it out in front of her. "And now?"

William looked into the mirror's smoky depths. His eyes widened as he understood what it was that he was seeing, what was looking back at him from the depths of his own reflection. His hand shook and the dragon dropped to the ground. He reached forward and touched his fingers to the face of the mirror.

"I saw a dragon," he said.

Margaret let the mirror slip down onto the floor. "If it, the Regent's Bridle, does what you say maybe that's what it means. I see it too when I look at you with that thing in my hand. Perhaps we see the dragon because you are descended from the Dragon King, Lukas. The Bridle is meant to say who is, but how does it show? How better than to show a man as a dragon? But then how can that make sense when Harild isn't legitimate? He isn't descended from Lukas...."

William bent and carefully picked up the Bridle. He put it inside the small pouch that hung from his belt. "Best we let Allen know about all this, and we can decide together what to do."

ᆨᆨᆡᆨᆨ

It was barely first light when the guardsmen came to Allen's rooms and banged on the door with enough weight and clamor to wake the whole house. Yarrow leapt to admit them but was just pushed roughly aside.

"Your staff will stay here and speak to no one," the first of the guards said. "You will come for us. It is the king's order, no delay."

"Might I at least get my cloak?"

"No."

Allen laughed but stopped as they seized him abruptly and dragged him from the room. He was taken not to the airy receiving chamber, but to an echoing room in the depths of the dungeons. They went by a long and winding way and Allen was not at all sure he would be able to retrace his path.

It was not a cell, exactly. Just a large space with walls made up from natural stone completed by patches of masonry and a vaulted ceiling. At its apex a grilled porthole admitted a single stream of light that splashed against the wall in front of him. Just below it and lit only dimly from above, was a figure on a carved seat. It was the king.

Allen felt a deep thrill of danger. Here he was in king's own dungeon—a place where he was absolutely in the king's control and if he were never seen again, so few would miss him. None who could confront a king on the matter. Allen searched his mind for any offense that he might have committed but nothing of substance presented itself.

"Tell me about William," the king said.

Allen was an ordinary knight and a few weeks ago he would have been happy to answer that question glowingly and in full.

Now he was suspicious and afraid of incriminating himself or William, or walking into some unforeseen trap.

"Do you think he follows the devil?" Harild added.

At that Allen let out a sharp involuntary laugh. "The devil, Your Majesty? No, William is not in league with the devil. He concerns himself mostly with the propagation of vines and the breeding of fine red-eared cattle. He is taking a little while to get used to having a wife, but that is only to be expected when one arrives so suddenly."

"Why, Allen, I do not remember you being so bold," Harild said, standing. His face seemed good-humored, but Allen knew that Harild was a cunning man and never revealed more than he intended. Allen did not want to offend the king, but his desire to protect William's good name was the stronger motivation.

"It is not every day the king implies my brother might be a minion of the devil, a circumstance I am sure might see him hung, drawn and quartered. So I don't meant to offend, but I would not want a shadow of a doubt to remain. I know William very well, and I will not hear a word against him even from you, Your Majesty."

Harild came forward and waved the guardsmen away. "Shut the door behind you," he said casually. "I would speak to Sir Allen alone."

He walked around Allen slowly, as they were left alone on the darkened cavern.

"You are rather loyal to the young man, aren't you?"

"He is my brother."

"Is that what he is? One hears of your habits and it does rather beg the question of the nature of the attachment."

Allen stiffened with affront. "My conduct is my concern. William is above reproach. He has never...behaved improperly."

Allen's mind went to the previous night. He was not speaking the whole truth to the king and when William had swayed towards him, all barriers fallen down.... It had been such a terrible temptation.

"No?" Harild replied wryly.

"No."

Allen stayed facing the empty chair as Harild circled him like a beast stalking its prey. He heard the king's voice clearly in the still, quiet chamber although his voice dropped lower and lower.

"They say he fought well, too well in fact for man who'd never but sparred in the practice yard."

"Can a man fight too well? Perhaps it's in his blood? Some men come to it most naturally whilst others will never even hold their own."

"What do you mean by that?" the king said sharply.

"His father was a knight, his father's father. That is why titles pass down families is it not, because talents also do?"

"More fire in his mother's blood than anywhere else," Harild muttered.

"Your Majesty," Allen said stiffly. "Whatever it is that you want from me, I am sure I shall be happy to oblige you. But perhaps you might disclose what that is exactly."

Harild was somewhere behind Allen now, his quiet voice echoing in uncanny whispers along the ragged wall.

"Oh but you do oblige me, Sir Allen, you do. You see, although your company may well have its charms, all I am interested in what William is capable of. So we are going to play a little hide and seek. You, Sir Allen, are going to hide. And we shall see, if William seeks you."

That last phrase was accompanied by the sound of a door scraping open, and punctuated at the end by it slamming shut. Allen turned and walked to the door with trepidation. As he reached it, the lock snapped as the key was turned and withdrawn. Allen wondered how long he would bide here. He had a terrible vision of being left to starve in this cavern with only the mocking window high above to keep him company. He shook that feeling off as best he could. Whatever the king's purpose, little would be achieved by that—and for all that Allen heard the king could be callous, it was never without good reason.

Allen was not looking forward to an extended stay in this damp pit of a place, but he was far more concerned about the king and his sudden fixation on William. William was a capable enough man but a minor knight without any great assets or influence. Allen began to wander the periphery of his prison, wondering just what it is that William could have done. It was a question William himself would do better to grapple with; it was he who could always answer the tutors' riddles and solve the creeping equation set upon their slates.

Allen wrapped his arms about himself as the chill began to set in. He dearly wished now that he'd had time to grab that cloak. He wondered if Yarrow would do as he had been commanded, or whether William would have at least a little advance warning of the king's strange behavior.

In the darkness, Allen thought of William and Margaret both, and recognized the depth of his yearning for each of them, not to the exclusion of the other but somehow in concert. He shook his head and continued on his hopeless search for some method of escape.

Chapter Twenty

Margaret waited in the garden. As William walked over to her, he appreciated the sight of her curvaceous figure beside the rose bushes, which hung heavy with great white flowers. It was possible to appreciate her beauty in the same way one admired a fine tapestry or painting. Possible, but difficult.

William lifted his gaze back to her face and forced it to remain there. There was a greater problem at hand than his muted passions. He had been contemplating his inevitable doom, yet the more matters developed, the more he began to wonder if he had misread the nature of the situation entirely.

"Yarrow says the king's guard came for Allen early this morning," William told her as he approached. "And said nothing about where they took him or why."

"Damn," she sighed. "What is he up to?"

William looked up into the sky, hemmed in on by stone walls on all four sides. He supposed she meant the king, although only someone raised in the royal household would refer to him so casually.

"I dare not approach the king until he summons me, but is there any way you...? I mean it has been hours now and I have to wonder why he had to speak to Allen so urgently and so early? I am...concerned."

Margaret pondered that for a while. "He never spoke to me, but Mother returns today, and he will still see her, almost on demand. I could wait for her in her room and ask as soon as she arrives."

Allen grasped Margaret by the arm. "Let Yarrow know how to find you so he can come and tell you if Allen returns."

"But what will you do?"

William raised his hands. What would he do?

"I will look for him, I suppose."

She didn't have to say it. How would he achieve anything in a place where few knew him and the king had almost absolute control. But he couldn't just sit by blithely and see how matters panned out—if there was any chance Allen might need him, he had to go to him. He had no allies in court, barring any his wife might have, and so very few options.

"I will start with Yarmoth, I suppose," he said. "He seems to have taken to me, albeit in a fairly patronizing manner. But he's in favor with the king, I hear, and might know something."

"Then should you be walking into his parlor?"

"Perhaps not, but there is a limit to what we can do bar wiggle a little in the king's clutches. I support I will wiggle, a little, and hope for the best."

"That's…"

Margaret fell silent, her pursed lips showing how little she liked the situation. "Perhaps it would be better if we stayed together."

"Yarmouth will not be frank with a woman present, nor will your mother speak freely if I am present. We must do the best we can, and meet again, here in the garden. Finister can wait in our rooms to ensure that we know if the king sends for us."

Margaret reached forward and hugged him quickly. "I will do my best. Take care, William. Take great care."

"You also."

"I also." She backed away with a smile.

William felt the warmth of her body against his fading. That was it, he supposed. Some time during the last few days he had definitely fallen in love with his wife. And now she would not touch him for fear they were actually brother and sister. He felt his mouth curl into a wry smile. In a way, it made his decisions clearer, because it was surely more virtuous to give up a woman you love than one you disdain. But his heart struggled to find new hopes. Somewhere in the impenetrable mess of circumstance, he was beginning to doubt the very foundation of his resolution.

Ahriman. Who or what, after all, was Ahriman? William scoured his mind and as far as he could remember. Although William had called the entity the devil, he had never answered to that name. And in a situation where magic was becoming commonplace, the fact that he had some stranger powers did not immediately beg a divine or devilish nature. Perhaps it was only wishful thinking. He did not grab at the possibility too eagerly for fear of raising himself to hopes that would only be dashed.

William turned towards the center of the keep, hoping to get to the north wing where the king's more favored courtiers lived in the relative comfort of the newest part of the castle. The king, for his part, lived in the oldest and most cramped rooms but would not be budged from them. It was cause for some comment, but if the king did not hold with tradition then who would?

He needed to pass through the general hall to reach the sand court and from there the great stairs that joined the east wing to the old keep. The hall was never empty, but its mood was rather different today. A cluster of dark cloaked men sat around the great fireplace. They had pulled the benches over in a rough semi-circle and William saw their hunched backs. They turned to watch him enter, a row of pallid, bearded faces. With a sinking feeling, William noticed they were facing toward a shabby figure that stood upon the hearth, apparently addressing them. It was Festrigan.

But this was a rather different Festrigan. He looked less like a kindly uncle and more like an ascetic priest. His eyes were sunk deeper in their shadowed recesses and his fingers curled in avaricious claws. Festrigan looked at William with a feeble but fiery glare.

"And this is he," Festrigan said in satisfied conclusion.

There was a quality to the men he addressed. The were dour and soberly dressed, these were not the gadabouts of the court. These were devout men, many ready to believe the devil acted directly in the world of men and that it was their job to foil his evil plans. William might once have seen them as righteous men, and perhaps they still were and it was only his perspective that had changed...

"Think you're going to speak to the king?" asked one of the younger men, advancing upon William.

He considered retreating; it seemed unlikely that these men would resort to chasing him physically though the corridors. But William was not entirely prepared to creep about in fear of them, nor was there another way to reach Yaremoth's rooms, all possible paths passed through this central hall. Throughout most of his life, William had taken a cautious path, but finally he felt the urge to seize control. He had felt similarly just before attempting to cause his own death, but this was an altogether a different feeling. He would be bold and use what advantage he had, no matter what their provenance.

William stepped aside, as the young man went past him and closed the door. He then noted how the other doors were closed and guarded. It was becoming rapidly clear that Festrigan had much less interest in God and the devil than he did in seizing the Regent's Bridle. Perhaps he was not even honest about it within himself, but the old man wanted the Bridle and he wanted the power of having it. Even the king would have to heed him then.

With a quick and possibly ironic prayer, William stepped forward boldly. He walked directly towards Festrigan whose eyes flickered uncertainly. William was sure he seemed a slightly more forceful figure unconfined and much recovered with rest and the support of his allies.

"That would be the king's prerogative," he said in mild reply and as reminder of their shared earthly authority.

One of the older men piped up. "Some things even the king needs to be protected from."

Festrigan stepped forward to intercept him and spoke more to the point. "Give us the Bridle."

"Give *you* the Bridle, you mean?"

"These men have listened to my words, and unlike you, they are virtuous enough to be swayed by them. The Bridle will be safe in our hands, protected from men like you, who might use it. I had wondered why you waited. But now I see. You want to do it here. You want to target the king, our divinely appoint leader, and seize control, as the devil's minion!"

It would have been ludicrous if the nine men present had not watched with such fixed and solemn attention. William had only one slight advantage—that if they believed Festrigan then they must feel some fear of William as a fiend with some kind if dark power... And of course that they might be right to.

"Give it to us now," one of them said.

William walked forward to the fireplace. It was not a terribly cold day but the stones held their chill and a fire had been set to fight it. William leaned casually past Festrigan and into the fire. He took hold of the largest, brightest coal he could from the center of the blaze. He was not entirely certain even as he did it that Ahriman had told the truth, but the fire felt only slightly warm to his touch. It was as easy as plucking a piece of fruit from a bowl and he felt slight guilty pleasure at the power.

William held the coal calmly, turning it to show the men around him. Their eyes widened at the sight. The coal glowered redly; just its edges began to show a dusting of white ash as it began to cool. It was impressive to see, even to his own eyes. He supposed that it was well past time he felt the advantages of his curse.

"I will give what I have to the man who will first take this from me."

He proffered the coal to the nearest man, who stepped back. He moved his hand in a slow arc and the others shrank away from him. He did not risk addressing Festrigan directly but hoped that daunting his followers would be enough. William walked boldly to the far door, offered the coal to the man who stood there. He stepped back, making a vigorous sign of the cross against his chest. William drew back the bolt and left, closing it gently behind him.

As he left, he chuckled slightly at the ease of his escape, but quickly his mood changed. He walked a short distance and stepped aside into an alcove where a fountain played. He dropped the coal into the shallow water where it subsided with a hiss into a grey mass and a cloud of floating scum. William curled his fingers over the rim and waited 'til the tremor in them subsided. He supposed that all men who turn to evil do so gradually and only learn to like it after a while. For surely he had enjoyed the fear in those men's eyes—and maybe all they wanted to do was protect the king for the devil's schemes. William could not afford to dwell on those considerations now.

"Allen first..." he muttered to himself. Somehow he felt if he could just get Allen back he could make sense of things somehow.

He heard a door slam and angry voices behind him. William knew he had just made a monumental mistake. He had only been thinking of keeping the Bridle out of Festrigan's hands, but instead he had handed proof of witchcraft to a jury of his credulous followers. Any man would believe him the very epitome of evil if they had seen what he had just done.

"Ahriman, damn it, where are you now? I need to speak to you."

"Do you just?"

Ahriman looked rather different. There was a luminous glitter to his eyes, his face seemed longer and the wings rustled in leathery folds. Thing began, quite gradually, to fall into place in the back of William's mind.

"Who are you?"

"Did you call me just to ask me that? Or are you finally finding a use for my little gifts?"

"As usual your gifts, as you call them, in combination with my own stupidity have made this situation even worse. I called you, I suppose, to ask you something. I do not expect you to answer."

William pulled out the Bridle and turned it in his hands. "This is important. I begin to see it. But I am not a wise man. I need my friends. I need to tell them about all of this, as I have demanded honesty from them. I need to know where Allen is."

Ahriman straightened. "Follow me."

William gaped as Ahriman went past him and walked breezily down the corridor past a serving man who showed no evidence of seeing him at all. William kept his fingers wrapped tightly around the Bridle and went after him.

The passed through the newer parts building, down, along, down, around, along, farther down. The stones were darker and smaller now, weeping milky moisture and smothered in mold and grime. Finally they came to a deep cleft in the building. It seemed like the point where the building and the mountain met. Ahriman paused and scuffed at the ground where a metal grate was recessed into the ground.

"Look closer," Ahriman said.

William watched him for a moment, then reluctantly knelt and peered though the grate. All he could see was a small patch of light against the wall. He became uncomfortably aware there was a large void directly beneath him which this portal overlooked. It was like a pit that someone had belatedly provided a grandiose roof for.

"Call out to him, William."

"Why are you being so helpful all of a sudden?"

"I have always had one guiding principle, William. I act on whim. Today it benefits you, tomorrow I may snuff you out."

William leaned down over the grate. "Allen?" he called in a broken voice.

"William?"

William's fingers curled around the ragged metal of the grate. As he stared, the small patch of light was broken. He could see the top of a pale-haired head and, as it turned upwards, Allen's face. William felt his heart make one of those thumps that were much spoken of in romantic songs but actually rather unpleasant to experience.

"William, what on earth are you doing up there?"

"Are you all right?"

"A bit cold and extremely bored. At the risk of stating the obvious, the king seems to be up to something."

William could feel the grate shifting slightly under his fingers.

"I have to get down there."

"Do you want me to help you get down there?"

William turned to a creature that had until recently terrified him. But now he did not feel that awe. Respect, certainly, and caution—but he could not stop himself from replying as Ahriman obviously expected.

"Of course."

Ahriman smiled. He leaned down, raised the grate and lifted it aside as if it had no weight. Without warning, he grabbed William and stepped forward into the void. William yelled and heard an answering exclamation from Allen. He flailed his arms, but continued to move only gently down into the darkness. He floated as light as a feather down to the floor.

His feet touched the ground and Ahriman stepped back. Allen watched, gaping from the periphery of the room. William reached out, just one arm towards him and Allen staggered back just like Festrigan's superstitious followers. Ahriman was laughing as if at a magnificent jest.

"You are," Allen said in a shaking voice.

"Allen..."

"The king knew, you are a witch, you have powers from the devil."

William straightened. "Well, that's a matter of conjecture."

"I...what?"

William looked around, scowled at the smirking face of Ahriman, and then turned to Allen. "Before you call for a priest, would you hear my, rather belated, explanation?"

Allen could be accused of many things, but cowardice was not amongst them. He looked long and hard at William, and quite perceptibly, he relaxed.

"I hope it is a very good explanation, William. But I shall certainly hear it. I suppose when it comes down to it I might do anything for you, even be damned."

He came back to William's side with only a slight hesitancy. "So how do we get out of here? And the king was waiting to see if you looked for me so he must be watching."

William looked around the room. It was dark and the door was obviously locked or Allen would not be waiting within so patiently.

"The door may be watched. Come here, to me."

He reached out to Allen.

"What are you going to do?"

"We will go back the way I came, with a little help."

Ahriman raised his eyebrow sardonically, but stepped forward.

Allen was daunted but he stepped forward. William put his arms around Allen and linked his hands around his back.

"Ahriman, if the whim continues to strike you, would you assist us?"

They floated upwards. William was beyond his first shocked reaction, but he sympathized with Allen who was quite rigid with terror. They landed in the small corridor. Allen's legs seemed quite weak and William held onto him as they landed gently on the floor. Allen sat with his back against the clammy wall and William leaned over him.

"It will be all right, Allen," William said. He leaned over impulsively and kissed Allen softly on those thin, delicate lips of his. "It will."

Ahriman replaced the grate. "That's quite enough lifting and carry for grubby mortals for one day," he said. "I am sure you can find your own way from here."

With a whisper of wind, he was gone.

William put his arm around Allen. "Come on. Let us go and await Margaret. Then I will tell you both the whole story as I know it, and I will tell you what I propose to do."

Chapter Twenty-One

William could not help but note how far away Allen stood. In fact, he wavered as if drawn by two conflicting currents, one towards William and one that repelled. Allen hovered near the window, and as if to have some reason for it, he pulled to the shutters closed even though the sky was only just beginning to darken. He spent some time setting the hook firmly in its latch and then turned to see William watching him with a fixed and solemn gaze.

"William, you have to tell me how the hell you could do that," Allen said. "Because I do not think you are an angel and I do not like to think that you are a warlock."

"Once Margaret is here I will explain."

"This is not some jest you don't want to spoil by repeating. Are you a follower of the devil, William? Have been in love this whole time with some evil..."

"I am not sure," William mused. He was rather satisfied at how calm in sounded in contrast to Allen's quavering tones.

"For pity's sake." Allen walked over to him and grasped him by the shoulders. "No," he said. "Even if you admitted it, I'd not believe it. Even if the devil himself told me so."

"I suppose that could probably be arranged." William smiled wanly. "I have been manipulated somewhat by some creature. Perhaps a demon, or a witch. I would think him just a delusion, but for the clear evidence, such as you yourself have just experienced. Your faith in me may be a little misplaced but I am glad you are here, for Margaret's sake at least."

"But did you make a bargain with this...creature?"

"After a fashion..."

"What, tell me! Tell me how to help you, what you have done?"

William tried to force out the words, but they froze upon his tongue. Even Allen could not believe what he had agreed to, whether the pact was with the devil with some other creature— whether the child's death was directly his responsibility or not. He had been willing to make an agreement that no tolerably virtuous man would and now Allen knew Margaret—knew the woman whose child William had so callously bartered.

William felt his breath go out like a slow tide. He reached out one hand and laid it against Allen's unshaven cheek. The stubble scraped against his palm as Allen waited for his answer. No matter how he put the pieces together, William did not see himself in the puzzle. Even if he was not going straight to hell, it would be better if, before all was over and done, he was gone. He could fight, after all, and there was always a need for mercenaries in the realm. The more he thought about it, the more he was sure of that necessity, and it made things easier. He had to act boldly to ensure Allen and Margaret were looked after.

"What would you do if I just admitted it?" William said. "If I said, sorry, Allen, but I'm a warlock. What would you do?"

"Don't, William. This...isn't you." Allen's expression tore at him, marked with doubt and fear. "The answer is that I'd still love you," he replied. "I'd do everything I could for you, and for Margaret. Even if I went to hell for it, William, you'll never have anything to fear from me."

"You love her too, don't you? Margaret, I mean. You don't need to lie to me about that. She is a woman any man might admire." Allen's gaze dropped down to the floor. "Allen, I will answer your question, if you will answer mine—and as truthfully."

Although a lie would serve as well, either way William would know.

"I could. On my honor I have done nothing to betray you. 'Tis just a feeling of my heart that encompasses you both. I cannot think it is a sin, to love as I do. I only wish I knew what you felt in return..."

William wondered what that meant about the vision he had seen of them together, for Allen seemed to be speaking only the truth, as he had so recently promised. It did not matter really, for Allen did love Margaret regardless, and so long as William could be certain that she returned that feeling his plan might yet bear fruit. But this was not the time to dwell upon it.

"No, of course not," he said, "I should hope that if she ever lost me, you would take care of her. You have little enough reason to feel loyal to your own family beyond what propriety requires. I had hoped one day... It is probably foolish to ask, for you come from a great house and mine is a very small and modest one, but I saw you, somehow, being part of it."

"William, we shall never let anything happen to you, any more than I would allow my errant feeling to come between you and your lady. Please stop talking like this, and tell me simply, what the hell is going on with you?"

"I'm not concerned about your feelings, whether you characterize them as errant or not, Allen. She may find what happiness she can. I do not think anything can ever truly come of our hasty and dare I say involuntary betrothal. I have done my best to make that clear to her, and I say it to you, also."

William felt Allen trembling beneath his fingertips. He leaned closer. He could smell tack soap and damp wool. He felt his breath in conspicuous gasps. Allen was so close to him and William only regretted all of those moments he had squandered, all of those times when Allen was close to him, so beautiful, so loving and so willing. He came to a strange and sinful wisdom just a little too late. He loved Allen with his heart and should have let his body follow. Even now he felt the pull, the desire of Allen's warmth so close before him in this lonely room.

"Allen..." William shook his head. "I am so sorry..."

And at that moment, the door crashed inwards.

ఞ✕ఞ

"I promised your father I would never disclose, not even by omission or exclusion, who he was. It is a predictably fraught matter, but then this is the royal court and the course of true or any other sort of love is inclined to be a little...devious. But Medry's conclusions must make some sense to you, dear daughter. As I recall you have a tolerably rational mind when you choose to employ it."

"The logic does not escape me, but I cannot be sure which you would prioritize, the king's schemes or your daughter. Nor am I foolish enough to think your promise binds you so much as your desire to retain influence and maneuvering space—the ambiguity of my parentage is useful to you."

Margaret did not like the way her voice sounded, as if she were a child whining over some minor matter, but being in the same room as her mother seemed to strip away all of her defenses. This was, after all, a woman who knew her all too well, knew her from a babe. Yet somehow Margaret had never fathomed her mother in return. True, Pinty had never done

209

anything to harm her, but help was offered as she deemed fit rather than according to Margaret's own wishes.

Pinty shrugged and continued to unpack her trunk, laying out a favored evening dress upon the bench seat beside Margaret. Its fine silk glinted in the warm afternoon sun.

"There is a ball tonight, dear, do you know? Well, perhaps you have not been invited. If you made more of an effort to be pleasant you might receive more invitations to such events. There is only so much that even I can do on your behalf."

Margaret had waited most of the morning for her mother to arrive and she had learned depressingly little when she did. That was hardly surprising. Mother had apparently been a cryptic specimen most of her life and she had taken to court like a duck to water. Even after their brief affair had ended, Harild seemed to find in her a fellow spirit.

"What is he up to, Matron? Don't pretend that you don't know."

She finally received Pinty's undivided attention with that. Everybody told Margaret she resembled her mother, as if this were a surprise. Margaret had never had either her appeal or her guile.

Of course the men of the court did not see her with her face screwed up in exasperation like this. It was an unbecoming aspect to her personality that only her daughter saw—which is to say, it was the real Pinty Weathers.

"Maggie dear," she said waspishly. "I have never pretended not to know what is going on. I simply don't choose to tell you. If you had spent more time with me and less riding around the countryside, I might have turned to you as a confidant. But in either case, you are my daughter and I have looked after you interests."

"Buy marrying me off to the king's actual bastard progeny?"

"Really, Maggie, you are hopelessly overt. Now why don't you go back to said progeny and make sure he is properly aware of you devotion before he learns the truth? I didn't manage to give you a useful illegitimacy, so you shall have your royal connection by marriage."

"He knows of the possibility that the king is his father, I told him as soon as I knew."

Pinty sighed. "Get out of here. I can see I shall have to take care of everything. And do try not to tell the dear boy everything or I shall not be able to confide in you at all. I'm told he is pleasant enough but most men are hopelessly direct, let alone one raised in the back of bloody beyond as he was. I had wondered why the king kept such a distance from the boy. He even forgave the dear boy's father decades ago. It has rather taken a weight off my mind to find out what he was up to."

Margaret left the room, trembling with annoyance, satisfied that Pinty's vanity had at least deprived her of anything Margaret might have told a more sympathetic audience. Margaret very much suspected that the Bridle was at the heart of all these schemes, whether Pinty knew it or not. Margaret knew her mother had a quick enough intellect but it did not extend to arcane matters.

Margaret trotted through the corridors, grasping her skirts in both hands. As she went, her fears curdled in her mind and grew rapidly. Her throat swelled with it as she broke into a run. She burst into their rooms, and found what she most hoped, a scene from a dream. William and Allen in each other's arms.

"Allen, William!" she cried. She put her arms around both of them.

Allen seemed startled to see her, but also relieved. "Margaret, William has something..."

A deep voice sounded from the doorway catching them all unawares. "Sir Allen, I did not expect to see you again so soon." It was the king's trusted guardsman and his colleague. "But never mind, this time it is Sir William the king wishes to speak to, this very moment and quite alone."

❧

William felt both Margaret and Allen clutch his arm as if they might physically hold him with them.

"Of course," William said quite calmly, and in truth he was not reluctant to go. If he spoke to Harild, knowing as he did truth from lie, he might divine what was going on regardless of the king's intentions. He stepped forward, tearing free from both of them. He turned and looked from Allen to William. "It will be all right," he said. In a low whisper, he added, "If there is trouble, flee. You should wait for me, and Allen can tell you why."

He looked to Allen, and said nothing more but merely nodded. With his gestures, he could still lie. And if the king was not set on destroying him and some peace could be made, he would explain then the subtleties.

As he stepped into the hall, the guardsmen crowded close on either side of him. They walked in silence along the winding path towards the king's private receiving chamber. It was an inner sanctum that only the most trusted and privileged usual saw, but William was under no illusions. The king's power was absolute, and from this moment on, anything might happen.

He was shown at last into a small and ironically cheerful chamber in which Harild waited, affecting the jovial expression of a benevolent uncle. He waved casually to a chair that faced his own and waited while William sat in it. Within a few moments, they were left alone in the room.

"Sir William," Harild said. "So tell me, is there anything you would like to say to me?"

William replied levelly but carefully. "It is you, sire, who summoned me."

"Shall I be specific in what you might tell me? I shall begin with some recent, relatively minor, but nevertheless intriguing events. Why don't you tell me how Sir Allen of Argent came to move from one of my more secure and out of the way storage chambers to your own chamber without...and now here is interesting point, without apparently using the door."

William felt acutely aware of the detrimental influence of Ahriman's little present at that moment.

"Have you made the acquaintance of Lord Serle's advisor," Harild asked with false courtesy. "Come recently to these parts, I believe?"

"We have met. I spoke to him recently. He told me you can handle hot coals without even wincing and I dare say he would suggest that you simply walked through the walls."

"Actually I flew, right up through that little window in the ceiling."

Harild threw his head back and laughed. "You are an interesting man, William. You are not afraid of me."

"But I am."

"Oh, why?" Harild asked blithely.

"Because you are powerful, and I don't know what your intentions are."

"You have something I want, and I have something you may want."

"You do?"

Harild seemed highly amused by their entire exchange. "What is it that you want? I imagine what I have to offer is better, but do go on."

"I want three things," William said. "I want my marriage to Lady Margaret to be legally annulled on grounds of non-consummation..."

"Really?"

"Really. I want my foster brother Allen to be listed as my legal heir. And I want to know why I am here."

William sat on his chair, his fingers clutching at the armrest of his chair. He waited rigidly for a reply. Harild made a great show of considering the matter. Time edged on inexorably.

"I will do this. If you will give me the Regent's Bridle."

"You may have it with my blessing."

"Do you know what it is?"

"Not entirely..."

William cursed. The truthful words had slipped out, as they were wont to do if he did not hold his concentration.

"What do you think it is, this item you have agreed to give me?"

"It is a key to a gate, and when you open it something comes through. Exactly *what* is open to debate, but it seems to me that you are the king, and if this is a matter for anyone, it is obviously a matter for the king."

Harild leaned forward and for a moment naked greed was as obvious in his eyes as it had been in Festrigan's. "Give it to me now," he said.

"What kind of fool would carry something like that around with him?"

Harild stared at him piercingly for some time. "Of course," he said. "You will want me to arrange those things for you first."
214

"Yes and I shall want proof, witnessed document. Your sworn and public word on the matter before a hall full of knights and noblemen."

"And what do you think I will do with the Bridle?"

William looked up at the king gravely and let himself speak the truth. "You will use it to secure your power and for your own aggrandizement—beyond that you may well use it to benefit the realm of Ordran."

Harild's veneer of affability faded away. "That may be a little more candor than I care for, but at least I know we may speak plainly to each other. I shall have it arranged and announced this very night, and I will have the Bridle by dawn. You will have it then?"

"I will."

"Well, then. Tomorrow will bring more news, and you may come to see me a little differently then."

William was looking at the king, but not truly seeing him. He was seeing Margaret's face, as it would be when she heard what he had done. She would see it as nothing more than a rejection. William tried to harden himself; she would have Allen to comfort her if only he could turn them away from him and towards each other.

William stared into the void he was creating where his life had once been, and wished he had enjoyed it more whilst he was living it. The Tor was a beautiful place; he was well off enough and well enough liked. He had been offered the love of two wonderful people and managed to reject both of them. William smiled; in short, he deserved the exile he was driving himself towards.

"Tomorrow then," he said, standing.

"Tonight also. There is a ball and you must attend it with your two followers. I'll ask you again how you managed that tidy little escape, and this time you will answer me."

William bowed, perhaps not as deeply as he should have, and retreated.

Chapter Twenty-Two

William was more nervous at the door to his own rooms than he had been in the king's chamber. He stood at the door some time, until he heard other footsteps in the corridor and then, not wanting to be seen dithering at his own threshold, he swung the door open abruptly.

The two people he most admired in the world sat in facing chairs before the hearth. Allen was leaning forward to hold Margaret's hands in his own. They look up suddenly as he entered but showed no signs of guilt; that was as well for he wanted them to openly own their mutual love, it would make his plans easier to enact.

"He wants the Bridle," William said preemptively. "The king knows of it, and he wants it."

"What will you do?" Margaret said.

He is the king. I shall give it to him."

"Is that wise?"

"It is after a fashion wise, and after a fashion foolish," William said. "He means to open a door into another world. I am not sure what will enter, but I think that it will be dragons. I think His Majesty is better placed to know and he does not fear it—he wants the gate open and he wants it very much indeed."

"Dragons," Allen said skeptically.

"Dragons or demons, or perhaps nothing at all. From tomorrow it will be in the king's hands, where it damn well should have been all along."

Margaret was beginning to stand but William walked over to them and placed a heavy hand upon her shoulder to hold her in place.

"Let me explain a little. He needs the key, a gate in the heart of the keep here and a person to go through the gate and open it. I leave to the king to know what to do. I don't doubt that the scholars of the keep know more about the damned thing than we do, and it is he who is meant to make decisions for this nation, not I."

"And if he chooses wrongly?" Margaret asked.

"Then we are all damned," William snapped. "But it will be out of my hands. Because, do you know where my concern lies? It isn't devils and mythical beasts. It is our own lives and those who depend upon us. What will you do, Allen? Wander from fight to pointless fight until someone finally ends your life? And, Margaret, you do not even know if you have been married to your brother..."

"No, William, my mother has finally made it clear that that cannot be the case..."

"The idea is there between us and will never been entirely gone." William pressed on without hearing her out. "And I know the two of you have feelings for each other. So I ask you, if I could make it possible for you to be together, wouldn't that be the best solution? If I could find a way to give Allen security and a stable livelihood? I ask you if you had not been given to a man you did not know, is Allen not the man, the kind of man, you would have freely chosen?"

"William, I don't feel that way for Allen," Margaret said.

218

The sensation of the lie was cold and wet, running down his spine. William shuddered but struggled to show no outward sign of his disgust at the untruth, for fear it would be misinterpreted. At least he had his answer now—when she denied her love for Allen, she lied.

"You do love him. I don't require you to say it but I assure you that I see no reason why you should not. Allen is good man, not unpleasant to look at and, beneath his sometimes-blithe manner, deeply caring. He is easy to love and I would be the last to deny it or blame you for it. Our hearts are not always wise in their inclinations, but there is much I can do to smooth the way."

He was careful not to look at Allen as he said this. William rested one knee on the ground and spoke to them at their seated level. He knew they were not going to be best pleased with what he had done, at least not at first. But in time, they would have to appreciate what he had done on their behalves.

"You two want to be together, you have love for one another. And there is a way for this to be allowed, openly and without embarrassment."

Allen leaned forward and put one arm around William's shoulder.

"I'll not protest that you are wrong, because you're not," Allen said. "But as usual you are blind to your own role in our lives. I have told Margaret how I feel about you, how I have always felt about you. She understands, William. Yes, we feel strongly about each other, but also about you. Why do you take such pains to put us together when we will not have it at the cost of you? Your wellbeing is foremost in our minds, and in our hearts, if only you will see it. Our love for you is the greatest thing that unites us and the source of any love we have found for each other."

William pulled back from them both. "There is no way in this world for two men to be together, let along two men with the same women. Show some damn sense, Allen. Of the three of us I am the one with the most options to exercise, as you shall see."

"What are you suggesting, William?" Margaret pleaded. "Allen tells me there is magic at work with you, not just from the Bridle, other magic, black magic even. Is someone making you act this way? Tell us everything and perhaps we might find another way. I can only suspect you are in danger and you hesitate to involve us; if you love us at all you should not hesitate. I would regret nothing, if only you gave me the chance to do what I think best rather than choose on my behalf."

"There is a creature who has been following me, perhaps it is the devil. I don't know." William paced the room, trying think how best to put them off without having to try to speak a lie and give everything away. "But I am not talking about me here. I want to know if I have done the right thing..."

"What have you done?" Allen asked stilly. "Just tell us what it is that you have done."

William backed towards the door. It was telling how Allen always spoke of he and Margaret as "us". It was enough. He looked down at them; unconsciously their hands sought each other out, Allen and Margaret facing him as a united couple. There was love there, he was sure of it. But if they picked away at his plans for himself, they would discover them, and that might destroy everything he planned for them.

"We are invited to the ball," he said. "You will understand then what I have done if you attend. All will be made clear then."

Allen was standing even as William reached for the door latch. William fled from them, down the stairs and into the dusk shrouded garden.

He curled his hand around the Bridle, wishing fervently to evade them. In answer to his need the shadows grew denser about him as he ran, and then with a sudden jerk, he was somewhere else entirely.

It was dark there, and a distant wind whimpered. As William's eyes adjusted, he began to see the rock walls and he thought for a moment that it was the room Allen had been imprisoned within. Gradually he began to see it was a larger chamber, carved entirely from natural rock and stretching out unevenly into the distance. It was possible even that some of that dark expanse was made of night sky, not encompassing slate. The cool air shifted in a way that suggested a natural opening somewhere out of easy sight.

Ahriman sat upon an outcropping of stone. He looked himself, and yet not himself...the changes was clearer now in that his form was part way between angels and demonic. His fingers were overlong and ended in talons and his eyes glowed with an angry warmth. His wings seemed larger now, and no feathers could be seen upon them.

"Who are you?" William shouted. "What are you?"

"I am not sure," the dragon said with disarming sincerity. "I think I am beginning to remember. I think I had to hide myself from a world cut off from my own. I could not even know who I was if I wanted to survive. I took on an appearance, an identity, that was not my own—waiting for the right man to come along. To open the gate is not difficult, but to have it opened by one fit to rule dragons... That took some time."

"Who are you?" William repeated desperately.

"I am Garwolf. When the gate was first opened from my world into yours, I was the first to go though."

"You are a dragon."

Even as William said it Garwolf's form began to shift and change. The very darkness seemed to writhe as his form uncoiled and splayed out into the great cavern. It was hard to even make out as William staggered back against the wall.

The dragon seemed to be made of the same black stuff as shadow except where dim light refracted off the edges of the scales as they shifted over each other, making soft sounds. Garwolf's head was the size of man's whole body; it stooped down to consider William. Its great golden eye became the only point of real light.

"Do you know the difference between a demon and a dragon, sir knight?"

William coiled his finger tight around the Regent's Bridle, feeling its rubbed corners hard against his pal.

"I think I do, sir dragon."

Garwolf laughed, a sound like distant thunder. "I am only just remembering myself, but I seem to have achieved my ends despite myself. A son of Lukas, the Regent's Bridle and the gate. Open it, William, open it and we shall go through together."

William gripped the Bridle hard, holding it against his chest. "I made a deal," he said. "I cannot do it, it is a task for the king."

"King? You are the king."

"I am not king, I have agreed to give this task, this honor, to Harild."

"King of men," Garwolf said distastefully. "You hold the Bridle, you are the king of dragons. Once the gate is open, dragons will come through and they must all obey you. Can you not imagine it? The great dragons in the sky and magic, true pure magic, all around them!"

The dragon's voice was beginning to rise.

"Tomorrow will be soon enough," William said dully. "And Harild will be king of men and dragon."

"Harild... There is nothing magical about Harild, no awe, no fear—he will rule dragons like other men would rule dogs."

Garwolf's great muzzle swayed, its very tip almost touched William hand. He could feel the warm air puffing from the dragon's great nostrils.

"I do not obey you yet, little man. The gate is closed. I am the greater of the two of us and could slay you with hardly any effort at all."

"And how would that help you?"

"Harild would come down here and have to get the Bridle from me, I could make my own bargain rather than abide by yours."

William had to admit that this was true, but it changed nothing. "You must do as you must do," William said.

Garwolf moved his sinuous neck, both yellow eyes considered William balefully. "I am a dragon again and this world has no place for me unless that gate is opened and magic from my home world enters to sustain me. I am a dragon now because you have made me remember what I am and if you do not open that gate, I will soon die. Open the gate, William, we lack only a man to go through it, everything else is ready."

Garwolf, then, did not suspect. William had no interest in being king of dragons. He lacked the judgment to be even an ordinary husband and knight. William was going to go through the gate and leave his two good friends without any obstacle to their happiness. In that one act, he would give them lands, title and freedom to cleave to each other. It was as good as being dead for once he went through he could never return. He needed Harild to use the Bridle. Harild would be the king of dragons and could then stay behind while William went through the gate.

৯৽৵

"Damn the man, he is harder sometime to fathom than the king," Margaret complained as she toyed with the collar of her finest embroidered gown.

"He thinks he is doing what is best," Allen replied, and he seemed quite certain of it.

"After all he has said about openness and honest, he has told us nothing at all. He wants to do what is best for us but cannot see that the thing we want most is to know what troubles him and have a chance to aid him."

"What can we do but see whether all is revealed at this ball? But it is getting late and there has been nothing but dancing and gossiping," Allen said. "I wonder if he sent us here merely as a distraction, to give him time to do whatever foolish thing he is doing."

They loitered at the edge of the hall where all the courtiers and guest milled in their finery. The music had quieted for a while and people drifted from group to group flirting and gossiping. Margaret and Allen stayed away from it, near the wall. Margaret saw her mother in the heart of the action and nodded. She received nothing more than an arched eyebrow in return.

The press of people seemed suddenly hostile. She gripped Allen's tunic sleeve with one hand, holding it like a talisman. He at least stayed by her, said and spoke his mind. For all that she loved them both, Allen was a easier man to love in many ways. Margaret shrugged her disloyal thoughts aside. If Allen said William acted only as he thought best, he would know, they were old friends and almost brothers. But if he did not trust William to act wisely out of these good motives, then that must also be likely true.

There was a sudden hush as Harild stepped up onto the small dais at the far end of the room. He raised both hands as he turned to the crowd. A party became in one moment an audience, and the king quite clearly had something to say.

"It is late I know," he said. "My guest of honor has chosen not to appear. But then he is obviously a young man full of surprises."

There was a murmur that rippled over the crowd as they realized something of import was about to happen, something few of them had seen coming. Pirdy scowled, she was not used to such surprises, and she cast her daughter a disapproving glare.

"I have three announcements to make," Harild said. "I know there has been talk. I am a man at my peak and I will not have it said otherwise," he smiled, giving people permission to laugh politely. "But beyond the peak, there are the years of decline and I am not so foolish as to deny it. I have no acknowledged heir, and for the stability of the realm an heir must be declared. He must learn the skills he will need to take the throne and make it his own. There are secrets, and pacts to be passed on. Therefore I am going to tell you all, I have chosen an heir. Not a man who has fawned upon me and whose only skills are in doing my bidding. That sort of man will never make a good king, a fit king for this great realm..."

There was absolute silence as the king paused and looked around. He put out one hand and a servant brought over a platter on which three documents were laid.

"I have had only daughters of my marriage but the cause of that lies not in me."

Many eyes went to the queen, resplendent in a white, pearl-encrusted gown and attended by two of her daughters whose haughty mien matched her own.

"I have a son, a son who has grown to be a man who is not cowed by his father, who lays his plans and sees them though, who is honorable and committed to this land. These next few weeks will be interesting times to an extent that I guarantee none will have foreseen. This is only the beginning of a new age for Ordran, only the beginning."

He took up the first parchment. "I have here a proclamation that the marriage of Sir William of White Lady Tor and Lady Margaret is declared annulled on ground of non-consummation."

He put that document aside and a clerk gathered it up as he raised the second document. "I have here a formal declaration that the knighthood and lands of White Lady Tor will pass entirely, at Sir William's death or by his declaration, to the knight errant, Sir Allen of Argent."

Margaret feel faint, Allen stiffened as all those who knew them by name and face turned to them. The implications were hard to grasp. William was casting them both aside, and she began to appreciate the reason.

"This final document states that I recognize Sir William as the son of my body and declare him legitimate heir to all that is mine to give. I do hope that if you see the young man, you will tell him of this. His two requests rather suggest he knew my mind, but he might be pleased to have the matter confirmed."

Harild's own gaze went to Margaret and he smiled.

Chapter Twenty-Three

Festrigan waited in the darkness. His followers would be there soon. He could see an infernal creature all but filling the center of the chamber. It was very still, perhaps sleeping. It was only natural to be afraid of such a creature but as he watched, it seemed like it was laboring even to take breath. Mayhap it was the virtuous air of a realm ruled by its God-given king. *Long may it suffer,* Festrigan thought.

He eased from foot to foot, hearing the sand crunch ever so softly underfoot. He had come in from the grounds through the cave. It wasn't too hard to find especially as he brought a few men with him to search around and find which of the caverns lead through to the gate chamber. It was also open to the sky so that a dragon could get in, or out, as needs be. He peered upwards but it was still pitch dark and clouded over without so much as a star twinkling. He had the three men with him, and the other two who went for Sir Allen. The rest showed a want of courage and held back. There was much to give them pause between the demon-gate and what might be beyond it and fear of their king who had been so seduced by the evil knight as to declare him his son and heir.

William's plans were proceeding well because he had been bold and forthright in his approach. Festrigan was prepared to learn from that and emulate it. He would step forward and play the best cards that he could put his hands upon.

There was nothing here but the demon and so he dare not move, not that there was any reason too. Festrigan was not so foolish as to think even once all his followers arrived that they could take on such as creature. Only the one who held the Bridle could command them. But he would be waiting. He did not doubt that William would arrive soon and have the Regent's Bridle with him. The fact that this creature was here made him worry that the gate was already open but it did not seem to be. Perhaps this one was a sentinel, awaiting the gate's reactivation? That would explain why it seemed so old, tired and worn. But it hardly mattered, once he seized the Bridle, he could close it and send the beast back before he did it. The devil's disciple might be bending the king to his wishes now, but Festrigan had a few tricks up his sleeve yet. One of them being a man in the guard who had let him know where William's own followers were.

The woman obviously meant little to him, but the man... Well, there were rumors. It seemed like pretty Sir Allen would be a useful hostage, so Festrigan had ordered him to be brought. He only hoped his men would have the sense to do it quietly. He sent the two biggest and staunchest men at his command and told them to bring Allen here, to the gate.

William came out of a concealed entrance, quite suddenly, and went to the head of the demon.

"Garwolf?" he said with concern.

The demon's eyes slitted, like golden crescent moons. "Hurry," it said in a great sibilant voice.

Festrigan stiffened as he saw the king enter wearing a thin nightgown and baring a naked blade. Thus garbed, Harild seemed faintly ridiculous, but he turned something in his other hand. It was a warmly-colored metal, shaped like a small beast of some sort. It must be the Bridle. Festrigan's gaze fixed on this, his prize. His hand tightened upon the rocks that gave him cover.

"This is actually Garwolf," Harild said with quiet avarice. "The first dragon to enter the world of men."

"And the last to leave," Garwolf bitterly replied.

The king must be under William's infernal influence, or he would not be so willing to deal with such a being—let alone seem to recognize its peculiar name. Festrigan hesitated to go against the king, but surely once the gate was properly closed again, he would be free of this evil spell and able to appreciate what Festrigan had done for him and the realm. Even if not, it would be worth martyrdom to stop these demons from invading the land. Festrigan thought of places where the Bridle might be lost, destroyed forever, but even as he did, his hands itched to hold it.

William saw the gate, a sullen bronze color at the far end of the room. It looked like a church door with scenes carved on it. It stood about a hand's breadth clear of the wall. The king skirted around Garwolf, who remained motionless but for his eyes, which tracked the movement. William could hear each wheezing breath the dragon took.

Harild went to the door and placed his hand upon it casually as if he had been there many times before. He took the Regent's Bridle and placed it in a niche at the very center, at the juncture of the double doors. It fitted into a carved scene in which a dragon and a crowned human flanked two bound figures—one, a man and the other, provided by the Bridle. The dragon fitted into the door as if it were cast with it in a single piece, seamlessly.

The very substance of the door seemed to shimmer and then with the loud crack, like a branch breaking in two, the door slipped slightly ajar and a watery light could be seen glinting behind them. The Bridle fell to the floor and the king stepped over it, raising his hand as if to...

"Wait," William said. "When you open it, someone must go through." He stepped forward. "If you are not careful it may take you, and once passed through, you could never return. Instead of a king here, you would be a slave there."

"Of course," the king replied. "But why did you hurry here without thinking of that? I had planned to...but who can we have brought here? Perhaps my doorguard."

"I did think of it—that man will be me," William said dully.

William stepped forward, quietly pleased at seeing Harild gape.

"Do you not know? I have offered you the crown, I have named you my heir."

"Have you?" William said distantly. "I am surprised. I would be a terrible king. I have no love for you and although I am loyal to king and country, I have no real interest in the realm beyond my own little corner of it—and even that is better in Allen's hands than mine. He is a proper knight, don't you think? He would never have done as I chose to do on his behalf."

"What are you talking about?" Harild snapped. "What kind of fool would choose, as you yourself have called it, slavery, over the crown I offer you? Perhaps I am wrong to choose you if that is the kind of imbecile you are."

William walked forward, his eyes fixed upon the glint crack between the two great doors. But then he heard a voice.

"William!"

Allen struggled between two large men in dark cloaks. All became clear when Festrigan stepped out from between the boulders to join them with two more thugs behind him.

"Whatever influence you hold over the king, I suggest you desist with it, hell spawn. If you want you *friend* here to live."

At that he drew a small dagger from his belt and gestured loosely in Allen's direction. William realized that although Festrigan had come to see the dragon and appreciate it for what it was, the others did not pay Garwolf any heed—they probably did not see his dim gray scales as even different from the surrounding jagged slate. They would not ignore such a thing so blindly had they seen it.

William looked at Garwolf's glinting slivered eyes. William bent and picked up the Bridle.

"What the hell are you doing?" Harild shouted. "Release him at once!"

The young thugs flinched a little at a direct command from the king and it was enough for Allen to pull free. He staggered away from them and collided with Garwolf's side. His eyes widened as his finger felt the regular pattern of the dragon's scales, and the slight heaving of his sides.

"So you're letting him open the gate," Allen snapped as he backed away from Garwolf. He actually tripped over the curling edge of Garwolf's tail but righted himself. "But who is to go through? Who is your sacrifice?"

"Where is Margaret?" William asked as he turned the bridle idly in his hand.

"They let her go, she may have gone to her mother, or even followed us knowing her...."

William tossed the Bridle lightly to his old friend. "I gave this to the king as I promised," he said. "But he seems to have discarded it. Now you have command of dragons, the land of the Tor and the love of a worthy woman. Try and forgive me for the rest."

He grabbed the door and wrenched it open. He caught a glimpse of steep and verdant hills and a sky turned indigo speckled with golden stars. Trees towered over the ravenous cliffs and the sky thronged with shadowed forms aloft. It was a glorious, terrible sight, but beautiful—so incredibly beautiful. He stepped forward without regret or hesitation....

A great taloned hand wrapped around his body from armpits to groin and wrenched him back. William cried out and reached for the gate, his finger barely touched the cool surface of the sucking portal, as he was snatched away from it. William could see his tidy solution, his new world, and his fresh start stolen away. "Sacrifice," he said. "Exactly. This is my chance, my only chance at redemption. To be, chosen, sacrifice. Do not prevent me from doing this."

"Now, Sir William," Garwolf said in a strong metallic voice. "I am feeling rather better with the gate being open and releasing the energies of my native land, and I am not entirely sure that I agree with your choice. So it is fortunate that it is not you that I must, for the moment, heed. 'Tis by long agreement that he who bears the Bridle is our king, whomever that might be and for however long..."

Festrigan's men cried out in fear at the rock coming to life. Their horrified eyes finally made the correct sense of the jumble of raged great forms that resolved themselves into Garwolf's body as he moved. Without hesitation, they fled. They might be righteous men, but the sudden appearance of an enormous hellhound has more than they could handle.

"Come back, damn you, you just need to get the..."

"The Regent's Bridle," Garwolf said, to complete Festrigan's statement. He moved fluidly, his long neck curving the regard them all. "Sir Allen, it seems I am yours to command. So tell me, little King of Dragons, who should be going through the gate, now that it is open? For it is open and if it is not fed soon, there will dire consequences. Leave it much longer and the better part of the keep might be what goes through the gate, and anybody in it. Choose quickly and it will be but one man, and he well and alive so long as he serves the dragon who currently rules our land, and holds the Bridle of men.

Allen looked around, taking in the increasingly fiery hue of the rippling gate. William struggled against the grip that held him firm. He cursed the intransigent creatures, he was too strong.

"It is my choice," he wheezed. "I want to go. You should understand why. It was you that drove me to it."

"Like hell," the king said. "Garwolf, I am king here and you will do as I say. Put my son down, give him to me."

The king seemed to think Garwolf might actually harm William, although all he had done was stop him from taking on permanent exile. Garwolf put his massive face down at Harild's level.

"He who holds the Bridle is my king." He swung his gaze in Allen's direction. "What say you, Allen? Perhaps Harild would like to go through this gate he has been so eager to open. It is your decision, but do not dither, time is passing swift."

"No, let it be Festrigan if it must be someone."

"Festrigan. I commend your choice."

William was set down hard on the ground. He stumbled, only dimly saw Garwolf's great talons snake out and snatch the old man, and toss him casually through the portal. The door creaked and slammed closed behind him. The cavern became dark as that mystic light was cut off.

"The others from dragon-lands will know now know that the bargain is renewed," Garwolf proclaimed smugly. "I wonder what sort of dragon will be the first to come through, and how many will follow."

He pushed William to his feet and prodded him in Allen's direction.

"How could you think of leaving us?" Allen said as he grabbed William and embraced him roughly.

"Indeed," the king added more waspishly.

William saw Allen blush at the king's gaze. He grabbed William's hand and pressed the Bridle into it. "He has the blood too. It is quite a disconcerting effect."

"Isn't it?" William agreed. He took the Bridle in his hand. He saw again the vision of a phantom dragon surrounding Harild. Now that he had seen the real thing, the simple illusion was not so daunting.

"That, I believe, is mine," Harild declared, he stepped forward with one hand extended, palm open. "I am king," he pressed, "and this is not more than what you promised me."

"I promised to give it to you and so I did. What happens now is another matter. And so you are king of men and by their consent," William replied. "King of dragons seemed to be rather a separate issue. It is Garwolf who should say who will have this damn thing... and I know I do not want it." That last said to Garwolf himself, who watched the goings on with evident amusement.

"Well, sadly it is yours all the same," Garwolf replied. "You have it, and I am content that you should keep it. So, dear king, what shall we do now?"

The great gate door shook and opened again. A figure stepped thought, its graceful lines etched in ivory tones. This dragon was not half of Garwolf's size but seemed to glow with life and its eyes glittered silver with inner magic. All eyes turned to this graceful vision as it emerged tentatively into the gloom of the cavern. Once its slender tail emerged, the door closed again behind it.

"Elder," the new dragon said as it went to Garwolf's side. William watched with some amazement.

If Festrigan had any kind of appreciation for beauty, the world of dragons should teach him that not everything that was magical was evil. There was a regal grace to the dragons that was beguiling. He turned, the Bridle in his hand. It seemed he had command of these great creatures, and that might just be enough to achieve what he had wanted all along. His title, his lands, his independence.

"Allen," he said, "you know what you have chosen?"

"I have chosen you. I am afraid I am not entirely sure what we should do now, but together I am sure we can come up with something."

Margaret scrambled down the stairway from the king's chambers. "We both have chosen you," she said. "And the dragons also. I think between us, we will find away to get a little peace, a little freedom."

In her wake came the door guards in their royal livery. She heard them and ran to Allen and William's side, pulling them away from the door and towards the dragons.

"How touching," Harild said as he turned to the guards. "Seize that man; he has stolen something from me. Seize them all and throw them in the dungeon. They are traitors. All of them."

William backed away from the armed men as they drew their swords, but they hesitated to come anywhere near the two great monsters that stood before them, regardless of anything the king might say. Allen stood to one side and Margaret the other but neither of them bore any weapons. William turned to the dragons.

"Garwolf," he said. "I would prefer that you stopped them, and that we got away from here. All of us."

It was the smaller dragon that stepped forward, coming between the king's men and their goal. "Stand back from our king," she said in musical tones that made her gender plain where her alien form did not. Garwolf raised his head weakly to watch her. Then he lurched to his feet, he planted one broad hand over the stairway. "Go gather your followers," he said. "We shall keep this king of men here until you are ready to depart. If he is wise, he will not force us to such interventions again. It is not wise for any man to start a war with a king of dragons."

"I made you my heir, William!" Harild shouted, red-faced. "Why do you throw that away? You could have had it all. King of dragons, King of men, king of an empire that stretches from the sea to the high ranges."

"I never wanted it all. I never wanted any of it."

The pale dragon settled down on her haunches to wait. "The best of them always say that, or so I'm told."

Garwolf laughed, a rolling rumble of contentment. Allen drew them away. "Quickly," he said. "Best we were gone from here."

"Hurry," Margaret urged. "Allen, to the stables and prepare. I shall fetch Yarrow and the others and meet you there. William... William!"

William turned to her, dazed by so many sudden turns of events. Margaret leaned up and kissed him lightly on the lips. "Don't just stand there," she said. "We are going home."

Chapter Twenty-Four

They rumbled down the road in the dead of night. Garwolf walked behind them and Ninieum flew overhead with all the vigor of youth, discovering a new world. From time to time her exclamations of delight could be heard as she swooped down to alight at some spot or another. William looked up at her with envy through the juddering window.

He felt cold, an all-pervasive chill. For a brief moment, he had felt the balance, their reckoning. He had been willing to sacrifice the life of his child; the only possible atonement for such an impulse would be to sacrifice his own life. He would have gone through into the world of dragons and left this world behind. Everything was accounted for, everyone had what they wanted, but Garwolf and Allen had prevented him, and known it was all wrong.

It would difficult now to bring his plans to fruition, but all was not yet lost. All he had to do was be the kind of man even the most tolerant of friends could not love, especially when they had each other to turn to. All he needed to do, surely, was keep himself busy and out of the way and matters would run their natural course.

ॐ

Ninieum lay nested against Garwolf's side. "Come fly with me," she purred. "The sky here is wonderfully bright and clear."

"Not yet," he said. "I'll have my strength back soon, then I will fly."

Ninieum was silent for a while. The she replied, "Who are you trying to lie to, Elder, me or yourself?"

Garwolf chuckled. "I have spent too long with these men who are so easy to lie to, and certainly I am much in the habit of lying to myself. But I do fear that it has been a strain on me, my wings don't serve me as they should."

He let his eyes close. The scent of crushed grass wafted in the air and the worm turn was soft beneath him. They rested upon a lush hillside overlooking the small castle of White Lady Tor. It was peaceful and the gate was still active, leaking dragon magic slowly into the world, but that would have little effect except near where dragons were to be found. It swirled around them and seeped into earth around them.

"In time you will feel better," Ninieum said. "The energies of our world will heal you."

"Maybe," Garwolf mused. "There is only the two of us, so far. That will reduce the strength of the magic that will build on this side of the gate. And I have been misshapen a long time. I am not sure how quickly or how completely that might ever be put to rights. Surely more will follow, more dragons would mean more magic..."

Ninieum shrugged and stretched out luxuriantly. "There have been very few dragons hatched in time since the gate shut. It has made our people more cautious. Very few go even to the elven worlds, or the dark lands, both of which are known to be rather more hospitable than the world of men. I, for one, don't regret it. When I saw the gate open, I acted on impulse."

"Do you regret your choice?"

240

Ninieum laughed. "No, the men and woman are not without appeal. But I cannot understand this new king of yours, what made you choose him."

Garwolf swirled his claws into the warm sod. "I didn't choose him exactly. He was the one I happened to be...well, paying attention to. Perhaps it was fate."

Garwolf looked down at the keep. Morning was fully broken and people could be seen working in the fields and moving about the buildings. Cattle were being moved to new pastures, a droving dog barked insistently as the placid beasts sauntered along blithely. Rugs were being aired on the balconies and hay was being cut, perhaps the last growth before the frosts.

"What I don't understand..." Ninieum said, as was very much her habit, "is why the king is rejecting his mates."

Normally Garwolf was happy to explain the vagaries of the human world, but this time, he was silent. It was taking him some time to go over the confused memories and understand what he had done. Much of it bothered him deeply. As a dragon, a long-lived being, he was able to consign the past to past, but William was very much in the present.

Garwolf turned his eyes to the far side of the valley. His vision picked out William and Shandrick where they stood watching the cattle file past. The herdsman stopped to speak with them. Garwolf could never understand the fascination they all had with the beasts; they didn't even taste as good as wild deer of the woods.

"As they count things, they are not mated," he said. "William thinks Allen should be Margaret's mate."

"But I thought she was already his mate, his wife."

"That was annulled."

"What does that mean?"

241

"It's not only that they are not married. Mated, anymore—but they never were."

Ninieum struggled with that one a while, a thoughtful frown sketched across her features. "That does not make sense."

Garwolf sighed and tried to think of a way of explaining the bizarre customs of marriage. He folded one clawed hand over the other, and rested his chin upon them.

"They were married which is a ceremony to show they intend to be mates, but as they didn't, it was...reversed."

"But he likes her, and the man."

"And so he does."

"Then I still don't understand."

"These people usually only have one mate, and he thinks that is better that Allen and Margaret be together."

"So why can't they be together with him."

"It isn't...usual."

Ninieum lifted her delicate head from the deep grasses. "And the real answer is?" she asked, looking directly at him.

"I was pretending to be some kind of demon, as you know."

"The great demon, the devil."

"I knew the child that Margaret carried was not strong enough and would soon fail. I simply formed William's affairs in a way so that it seemed like he had chosen to kill the child. I knew that to live I had to forget myself, and so I made myself into the demon. My goals were simply to stir up trouble in the house of Lukas, to drive men to desperate acts so that eventually one of them would open the gate in mad grab for power."

"You made him think he killed the child."

"I have told him that it was only an illusion, a trick, but that does not change what he chose to do."

"He changed what he has done. He should be grateful things were not as they seemed."

Garwolf watched as Allen went out to William's side. They spoke only a short while before William turned and walked away across the fields.

♥⋘

Finister and Margaret poured over the livestock records and accounts that covered the table in front of them in a tessellation of journals and loose papers.

"William is right about one thing," Margery conceded. "The stores are very low and winter is almost here. Now that we cannot depend on help from anyone else, things are going to become rather difficult if the season is harsh."

Allen came into the chamber. "Now it is the hay he must inspect in case the sun has dried it too far before cutting."

"If that is the case the cattle would starve, Allen. It is hardly a trivial errand."

Allen's jaw clenched as he sat down at the table opposite them. "It never is a trivial errand. The first frosts will arrive soon and everything is in chaos. Everything including our William for whom the frosts have come early."

Finister raised one eyebrow and absented herself from the room. "I shall just check these grain store records," she said. "They seem a little optimistic."

"Allen," Margery sighed. "We are here by his invitation and his sufferance. What can we do? If he wishes to devote his time to the estates..." She felt her voice drop, betraying her real feel

243

feelings. "Neither of us have anywhere else that we can go, Allen. The king stops just short of accusing us of treason and only the dragons make us safe even here. Harild could not send an entire army against them with any surety of success."

"Harild will have to swallow his pride and let the matter rest," Allen replied blithely.

"Perhaps he will, outwardly. But if we leave the Tor, we will not be safe."

Allen reached over the table and put his hand over hers. "In truth do you want to leave here, Margaret? Say that you do and I'll go with you. Let William spend a winter here on his own and see how it suits him."

"You don't mean that, Allen," Margery chided.

"How many times must I let him brush me aside and order me around as if I were his lackey?"

"He does not..."

"It certainly seems as if he does... Oh, Margaret. I do know he's still in there somewhere. But all he does is tell me to go to you. He is so fixed in seeing us together. But if he thinks he has achieved that end he will leave us both. The proclamation of descent is lodged and if he goes, this place—dragons I imagine included—becomes mine. But he wants to ensure that we are together so that it becomes yours also—all in one tidy package. That it why he labors to ensure that everything is ready to see us through the winter. So that he can go."

Margery knew he spoke the truth. "What is it that drives him? Is it that he will not tolerate one of us being left alone? We are not so feeble as to be unable to endure it, and find our match elsewhere, given time. Or does he know and repudiate what he truly wants; the three of us together? Ninieum tells me he is drawn to us both, but there is some other matter he does not speak of. That is the knowledge I would have."

"Ninieum," Allen mused. "She has been a boon. Watching over the land, caring for Garwolf, I worry about him when the snows come. She told me how William has powers from the dragons—to know the truth, to tolerate fire. But being human there are other effects. He cannot lie. So if only I can get an answer from him, I will know it to be the truth."

"It would also be a fine change from these moody silences. What is it you are proposing?"

Allen shook his head. "The best I can suggest is that we have Garwolf tell us William's troubles, his reasoning and then we confront him. Once he realizes for certain that we are staying with him, part of his life, and not letting him leave..."

"If we push him, there is no telling what he might do."

"What can he do? He must leave the Bridle and the dragons here to protect this land. If he leaves alone there is no place the king could not find him."

"There is one place," Margery replied. "One he has already tried to go."

"I'd follow him even there if you'd come with me."

"What kind of fools are we?" Margery said with a laugh. "I'd go with you. Even acting as he is, I love him. But I would love him better if only he would embrace the life this place can offer him, and all of us. I suppose your plan is no worse than mine."

"And which was that."

"A few bottles of wine and a subtle seduction. He watches us, and being offered what he truly wants, might not refuse it."

Allen raised one eyebrow. "Unsubtle, but perhaps sufficient. But which if us would be the better bait?"

"Why both, of course. We should begin as we mean to go on."

Margery sighed. "So you learn the truth of his concerns, while I see what is in the cellar. Let us not narrow our options."

⚜

William ground the rough strands of the standing bales between his fingers. A chilling wind was coming down from the hills and ruffling the shorn heads of the grass. The bales would be taken into the barn by evening but they weren't the best. They should have been cut earlier in the autumn when the goodness was still in the grass.

It was bad enough that he had been away, and Shandrick—but Shandrick's son had run off somewhere and nobody would say a word about it. Things had to be put to rights and properly stored or the household would starve when the snows came.

He hiked to the top of the paddock to see if the bales there were any better, but if anything they were worse. The hedge there was growing out and needed resetting too. William looked back towards the keep, he had come a long way, and drifting from task to task and the buildings were small in the distance. It was cooling as the afternoon progressed and the wind made the tattered collar of his workday tunic flutter against his neck.

A light ran began to fall and William scowled up at the sky, as if it cared about his opinion on the matter.

With a shrug, he headed back to the keep. He knew that by the time he got there he would be soaked through and chilled to the bone. Worse than that, his friends would be waiting for him. Despite his best effort to leave them alone together, they remained stubbornly amicable rather than amorous, except towards him. William could not bring himself to do more. Perhaps he should merely leave them to it. Matters were in a poor but tolerable state at the keep. His presence was the only real obstacle.

He saw Ninieum aloft again and wondered idly whether she was in any danger from lightning. There was no telling whether lightning was to be found in her world, but if it was a peril to their kind, Garwolf would surely have warned her.

She swooped down out of the sky and landed lightly just down the slope. The tip of her wing hovered over his head, holding off the rain, as it grew more insistent.

"I'll give you a lift the rest of the way," she offered with an outstretched taloned hand.

"I'm not really so keen on being hand luggage for a dragon," he said nervously.

"It will be pelting down very soon," she said. "Besides, I can take you directly to that drafty loft you like to call your bedchamber."

The chance of bypassing another awkward scene with Allen and Margery was a temptation. But there was something about the broad expanse or her reptilian face that suggested young Ninieum was up to something.

A yawn stretched William's face. He had been up since long before dawn and well-occupied all day. If the dragon was prepared to save him a long walk, it would be discourteous to complain.

"I would be most obliged," he said with a bow.

৵৹৵

Ninieum set him upon the high balcony with utmost delicacy. William was a little more shaken than he expected by the experience of being born aloft, and he barely managed to smile his thanks as he ducked gratefully inside his own small chamber. He was rather distressed to find Allen and Margaret both sitting upon his bed with an open bottle of wine, somewhat depleted, propped up between them.

"Ah," Allen said. "At last! Help us finish this off. A little of the grape does wonders for a man's sleep."

"I told you not to come in here," William said tersely, irritated to be bearded in his den.

But in the back of his mind, he saw a chance. Send Allen and Margaret on their way a little tipsy and nature might finally take its proper course.

"Come, William," Margaret said, patting the space between the two of them as she lifted the bottle aside.

William dithered, but his legs ached and his mouth was dry. He settled back against the headboard. Allen sat close by his left side, but took no advantage. Margaret to his right leaned in only slightly as she passed him a clay goblet. William took the cup and sipped from it cautiously. It was one of the better pressings, fresh but just starting to soften with age.

"I was just telling Margaret," Allen said, "of that time I went missing for three whole days and you managed to convince my father I was still in the keep. When the town guard finally worked out who they had arrested, my father told them they must have it wrong because I had been at home all along."

Oh yes, Allen had been the wild one of the two of them. "Of course," William added, "you got to have a wild time at a bordello. I just got to scramble to cover up, and then we both got the same punishment."

"Ah yes, but you got me back. Remember that time..."

It was just too easy to fall into reminiscence, and somewhere along the way William lost track of who was getting whom drunk. His cup was refilled so often and there seemed to be more than one bottle somehow. More than two. A single lamp at the foot of the bed illuminated the scene with a low, orange glow as all color drained from the sky.

"...but a girl never gets up to the same things a boy does," Allen protested.

"Really?" Margaret replied. "I once snuck into the king's chamber on a bet—and then got stuck there when he came in with his latest mistress. Quite an education it was for a girl. I couldn't sneak out 'til they both fell asleep near dawn."

"Oh," Allen leaned across, "what did he do?"

"Well, Melissa was certainly a forward minx. As soon as she got him onto the bed, she reached up..."

She demonstrated a gesture that crept up William's thigh with firm, probing finger, pushing up the hem of his tunic. William flinched back against Allen's arm, which had inveigled its way around his shoulder.

"Margaret," William warned.

Allen leaned over to him. "William," he whispered. "We have spoken to Garwolf and know what a trial he was to you, and how you blame yourself for your choices..."

William felt the weight of this guilt settle on him, and it seemed like Margaret saw it on his face.

Leaning into him, she said softly, "You thought you were offered only two choices. In the same place I cannot know what I would choose—but knowing and loving Allen as I do. Perhaps it would have been the same as you. I ask you, William, forgive yourself or not—as your conscience wills it—but do not think I blame you for it. We, all of us, make choices we would unmake if we could—but God does not give that option—and we must move forward. Can you not look forward and see a life with us worth striving for?"

She leaned forward and in a gentle gesture kissed him on the lips.

"How can I ever have deserved you?" William said. "Either of you. How would I ever be the kind of man to deserve you?"

"Oh, William," Margaret chided. "That's for us to say and you don't have to question it so much. We are, neither of us, fickle."

Allen replied more lightly. "Margaret and I agree that there is only on thing about your conduct that truly exasperates us."

Margaret's hand moved over his privates, and William replied quite hoarsely, "And what is that?"

Margaret replied for them. "That you refuse us, when you obviously care for, and desire, us both."

"But you two should…"

William's words were cut short as Allen kissed him deeply. William's eyes closed as he felt the warm mouth move against his own, tongue softly probing. They pressed against him on either side.

"Trust us on this," Margaret said gently as she took him in hand.

ৼৣৢৢৣৡ

William usually rose at dawn, but today he was not inclined to. Margaret spooned up against him, her soft body as warm as the first rays of the sun. Allen's arm lay over both of them protectively. William's mind was devoid of its usual busy thoughts. It felt *right.* His land, his lovers. He smiled as he curled back down under the covers, feeling skin against his skin on either side. In the distance, he heard Ninieum greet the day with her surprisingly unmelodic bugling call.

William had accused himself of many sins and some he was even guilty of but this, this was not one of them. King of men, he could have been—but he never wanted power. King of dragons? Only time would tell what that would mean. But beloved of two people who should have had more sense than to pursue a feckless scholar who made a barely passable knight... From now on, he could only hope to deserve that, highest of honors.

About the Author

To learn more about Emily Veinglory, please visit www.veinglory.com. Send an email to veinglory@gmail.com or join her Yahoo! group to join in the fun with other readers as well as Emily! http://groups.yahoo.com/group/veinglory

Look for these titles

Coming Soon:

Father of Dragons

hot stuff

Discover Samhain!
THE HOTTEST NEW PUBLISHER ON THE PLANET

Romance, fantasy, mystery, thriller, mainstream and
more—Samhain has more selection, hotter authors, and
everything's available in both ebook and print.

Pick your favorite, sit back, and enjoy the ride!
Hot stuff indeed.

Samhain
publishing ltd

WWW.SAMHAINPUBLISHING.COM